Mysterious America 2

MIDNIGHT PASS

Bill Thompson

Published by
Ascendente Books
Dallas, Texas

This is a work of fiction. Where real people, events, businesses, organizations and locales appear, they are used fictitiously. All other elements of this novel are products of the author's imagination. The author has represented and warranted full ownership and/or legal rights to publish all the materials in this book.

Midnight Pass

V.1.0

Published by Ascendente Books
ISBN 978-17355661-9-1
Printed in the United States of America

Books by Bill Thompson

Mysterious America
SERPENT
MIDNIGHT PASS

The Bayou Hauntings
CALLIE
FORGOTTEN MEN
THE NURSERY
BILLY WHISTLER
THE EXPERIMENTS
DIE AGAIN
THE PROCTOR HALL HORROR
THE ATONEMENT

Brian Sadler Archaeological Mystery Series
THE BETHLEHEM SCROLL
ANCIENT: A SEARCH FOR THE LOST CITY OF THE MAYAS
THE STRANGEST THING
THE BONES IN THE PIT
ORDER OF SUCCESSION
THE BLACK CROSS
TEMPLE
THE IRON DOOR

Apocalyptic Fiction
THE OUTCASTS

The Crypt Trilogy
THE RELIC OF THE KING
THE CRYPT OF THE ANCIENTS
GHOST TRAIN

Middle Grade Fiction
THE LEGEND OF GUNNERS COVE

THE LAST CHRISTMAS

This book is dedicated to my son Ryan and grandson Jack, who accompanied me on a fact-finding mission to Everglades City that culminated in this tale.

We explored the little fishing village, took an airboat ride, and ate lunch at the Havanna Café on Chokoloskee Island. We also drove the roads that led south out of Everglades City, looking for one that might lead us to a coastal town where every living soul perished one awful afternoon.

And after some searching, we found it. We went to Midnight Pass, just as you will, in our imaginations.

"I wouldn't go back to Midnight Pass if you paid me. Old-timers claim it's a cursed place—a place the devil chose to work his pleasures. Satan rode the hurricane into town that day and slaughtered every living soul. He left no survivors—not even a child. That's why people say Midnight Pass isn't in Florida...or even in America. It's in Hell."

Ed Hawkins, Chief of Police
Everglades City, Florida

PART ONE

THE MISSING

CHAPTER ONE

June 1988
Southwest Florida

Tom Horton hadn't been the first to disappear. Down in that part of Florida, persons went missing now and then. Some of them did it on purpose—people looking to check out and begin anew. Over the decades, several had vanished near a long-forgotten place called Midnight Pass. Tom was one of those. Not a clue of their whereabouts ever turned up, and each report became a cold case after a while. Nobody ever took the time or had the interest to determine if there might be a connection.

On the morning after Tom failed to return his rented boat, the Coast Guard had found it drifting in the ocean west of Naples. They accessed his GPS to track his route during a brief but intense thunderstorm that arose four hours after he left Everglades City in the twenty-seven-foot craft. He'd been three miles out in the Gulf but made his way toward land when the wind and rain started. He hugged the marshes until he came to the broken-down pier at Midnight Pass. From there, his boat had drifted aimlessly, tossed by winds and waves, leading the authorities to assume by then Tom was no longer aboard. Might he have abandoned ship in the storm or have been tossed into the sea? Searchers found his lifejacket on the beach, but there was no sign of Tom. Whatever became of him, no one knew, and after combing the town itself for clues, investigators gave up. Eventually, his case file would end up in long-term storage.

A seventy-year-old CPA from Atlantic City, Tom had taken some time off during a conference on Marco Island to try his hand at fishing in the Gulf of Mexico. His friends back home had suggested going to a tiny coastal town called Everglades City, the last inhabited place before thousands of acres of swampland that formed the southwest part of Florida. There, he could rent a boat and go snook fishing, which his buddies promised would provide a day of fun and entertainment.

When Tom rented the boat that morning, the weather was clear with light westerly winds. He was alone; he had a boat back home and was comfortable operating the craft, and so far he'd spent three enjoyable hours catching and releasing the spirited game fish. Around one, while he was having a sandwich and a beer, he noticed a sharp wind shift. The guys at the dock had advised him to keep an eye on the weather—afternoon storms could pop up without warning in south Florida, and some intensified quickly. Whitecaps from the swelling waves formed around him, and his boat began to rock, gently at first but growing stronger every few minutes. The skies darkened as the wind whipped his shirt. He stowed the gear, donned a poncho and a lifejacket, and radioed his position to the dock in Everglades City. He was an hour south, and he estimated it might take twice that long to get back, given the swells and the powerful gusts pushing him eastward.

Ordinarily he would have hugged the shoreline, but

this part of the Everglades was nothing but a marshy mass of sea grass that offered no protection. He pushed the engine for all it was worth, struggling to keep the boat on a northerly course as rain fell. Light at first, within minutes the drops pelted the canvas top like a volley of gunshots, and visibility dropped to just a few feet. Engulfed in fog, Tom kept a close eye on his chart plotter and GPS and prepared to ride out the storm. These afternoon downpours usually lasted an hour or so, and he hoped the winds would die down soon.

He pushed northwards each time the sheets of rain abated, but twelve miles south of Everglades City, a sudden gust sent buckets of water cascading into the small craft. It listed to starboard and took on more water as Tom struggled to right it. Just as he did, the clouds lifted for a moment, and he saw the remains of an old wooden pier just ahead. In shambles now, it had once been a large dock, maybe part of a marina or a restaurant. Despite its condition, the huge timbers jutting out of the water offered safety—a place to secure the boat and wait for the storm to pass.

As the bilge pumps struggled to get ahead of the water inside his boat, Tom pulled alongside one of the huge posts and cut the engine. When he stood to tie off the boat, another gust tipped it, sweeping him into the water. As the boat drifted away, Tom kicked off his shoes and swam thirty feet through the rotting timbers to the shore. Thankful to be on solid ground instead of swampy marsh, he collapsed on the sand, drenched and tired.

An army of sand flies swarmed around him, and he stood, swatting them off as he looked around the area. He'd lost his phone, and he walked away from the shoreline and up a tall dune, hoping to find a house nearby where he could get help. His heart raced as he saw a rusty wrought-iron fence a hundred feet away, its ancient spikes jutting skyward, separating the beach from what appeared to be an abandoned town. He walked to the fence and saw a sign hanging from an arched gate by one chain. Two lines of letters were carved into weathered, faded wood.

Welcome to Midnight Pass. Established 1896.

Someone had crudely carved a third line beneath.

Died September 3, 1935.

Tom walked through the archway and into what remained of the town. Both sides of the dusty street were lined with buildings in varying stages of decay. He walked past hulking shells with collapsed second floors, bricks and rotten timbers lying in the road, and yawning windows exposing dark, forbidding interiors.

Midnight Pass Hardware. Cotton's Bait and Tackle. Maloney's Tavern. Pete's Furniture. Goodland Five and Ten.

He read the rotting signs as he strolled past the buildings, and he thought about what he'd seen back at the fence. *How could an entire town die on a single day? Where did all the people go, and what made them leave?*

The storm ended as quickly as it had begun, and Tom heard a sound wafting on the breeze—music coming from somewhere down the block. Not just music—a very familiar oldie—"Venus," one of Frankie Avalon's biggest hits. As he walked and the music grew louder, Tom sang along with Frankie, because he knew every word by heart. It was weird hearing music in this long-dead place, but the song that played—his favorite sixty years ago—brought not just memories but a sense of dread. Something about this place just wasn't right. Not at all.

Two blocks down, he noticed a building and stopped dead in his tracks.

How could this be possible?

In a ghost town filled with rotting, spooky hulks, one edifice stood in the middle of the block, its red and white stripes fresh and bright. Although he hadn't gotten close enough to read it, he knew what he'd see on the sign above the door. He dodged debris to get closer and looked up.

Sweet Shop.

Double doors stood wide open, inviting...well, no one, actually...to step inside as Frankie belted out the chorus of his hit record.

I know this place. It stood in Atlantic City, down on the boardwalk. We'd all go there after school and listen to music—to this song, my favorite. But how is it here? Where on earth am I?

Tom shook off the chill running down his spine, walked to the entrance, and stepped across the threshold into 1960. The counter was there, and the seven swivel stools covered in red vinyl. There was a milkshake machine and a Coca-Cola clock on the wall that read 2:37 p.m. Tom looked at his watch. Yep, that was the correct time. But was it today's time, or the time on another day in another place? Seeing no one, he walked to the Wurlitzer jukebox that stood exactly where he remembered it. The first time he did the Twist had been on this tile floor in front of this machine...but of course, that couldn't be true. This wasn't Atlantic City in 1960. This was Midnight Pass, Florida, sixty-two years later. So how was this possible?

"Hi, Tommy. Didn't notice you come in!"

Startled, Tom whirled around and saw a man standing behind the counter—a familiar face, wearing that same apron and white paper hat and sporting that same moustache.

"Mr., uh, Mr. Callahan. Am I dreaming? How can you be here?"

The man guffawed. "This is my place. You know that. Where else would I be? Now what'll it be, son? The usual strawberry malted with whipped cream and a cherry on top?"

Tom raced across the room, put both hands on the counter, and leaned in until his face was six inches from the man's. "What the hell's going on here? How do you know that? And my name's Tom, not Tommy. I haven't been Tommy in…"

"You having a bad day, son? You don't look so good. I'll get to work on that malted; that'll make you feel better in no time." He turned and reached for the ice-cream scoop lying in its usual place by the sink.

Frankie stopped singing, and Tom turned to the jukebox. He watched the 45 rpm record eject and the arm rise to insert another. The next one slipped into place, and a song began.

"Venus if you will…"

The same song, but a different record. He'd seen the change. Perhaps there were two of the same title. He ran across the room, stared into the guts of the machine and looked at the label, but it spun too fast to read. A row of buttons ran along the front, and one—the current selection—was lit. "Cathy's Clown" by the Everly Brothers. But that was wrong, because the music was something else—his old favorite.

"What's wrong with this machine?" he shouted. "What's wrong with everything here?"

The man ignored his questions and asked, "Will Patti be along shortly? Should I fix her a chocolate shake?"

He screamed, "Dammit, Patti's been dead for twenty years. How do you know what we ordered? It's been so long…"

Mr. Callahan laughed. "Only since yesterday afternoon. You all came in after school, remember?"

"No! No, I don't remember! That's not possible. I'm not in school. Yesterday afternoon I was on Marco Island at a conference. What the hell's going on?" He flew into the street, cursing and shouting, and he ran and ran. Not knowing or caring which direction he took, he soon found himself on another block of crumbling buildings.

Crumbling, except for one. In the middle of the

block, a gleaming marquee extended over the sidewalk. He recognized it immediately, because he'd been there a hundred times as a youth.

Ritz Theater. The marquee displayed the name in a dazzling array of colored neon tubes flashing in sequence. Tom stumbled toward it, unable to process the overpowering wave of nausea and fear. This was another place from his past, and when he read the movie poster displayed next to the entrance, he fell to his knees, unable to catch a breath. A cold, dark feeling crept into his brain as he looked at his own face staring back at him and read the title of the film.

NOW SHOWING. My Life and Times, starring Thomas Horton.

CHAPTER TWO

What's happening to me? I'm in the movie theater, but how did I get to my seat? I don't remember walking through the lobby or the box of Good and Plenty candy in my hand that I must have bought at the concession stand. What the hell is going on? Did I die in that storm? Is that what this is about? Am I in Heaven...or Hell?

The screen lit up as a black-and-white clip began. *Newsreel,* the news of the world that always preceded the movie back when Tom was a kid. The words careened around his brain as he struggled to process the situation. He stared at the screen, more confused and worried by the minute.

This week in June 1960. The United States is sending its first troops to southeast Asia to assist in the five-year-old Vietnam War. A new dance sensation called the Twist is sweeping the nation, and a boxer named Cassius Clay wins an Olympic gold medal.

When the news ended, Tom viewed the short cartoon he knew came next, and then the feature film began. His senses dulled, he settled back and watched home movies from his childhood. What would have been nostalgic and fun in an ordinary world frightened him so much he held himself to keep from shaking. Numbly he sat through short clips of his life that no one could have recorded—his marriage, first job, birth and death of a child, the day he lost his Patti, the slog of daily routine in his career—and he leaned forward in surprise when he saw himself rent the boat in Everglades City that morning. He watched the boat being tossed in the wind, saw himself tumble overboard and collapse on the beach, and followed his own footsteps through the wrought-iron archway into Midnight Pass. He threw a fit in the Sweet Shop, stumbled down the street and walked into the theater. A girl behind the counter—Linda, yes, Linda, the same girl who worked the concession booth way back then—handed him the box of candy. Then he went inside and took a seat, and the news of the world started.

At that moment, the film stopped with a whirring click-click-click sound from the projection room. On the white screen was an image of 35-millimeter film with little holes running down each side. The film had broken, the way it sometimes did long ago. The projection operator would have to rewind it and start back up. But in his mind, Tom knew there would be no rewind, no restart, because he'd seen his life story up to the minute. There was no projection operator; he was alone. The screen was white because the past had ended. This was the present, the here and now, and Tom began to cry as he wondered what *here and now* meant in Midnight Pass.

Alone in the theater as the house lights came up, Tom exited and started walking back in the direction he'd come from. A block down, he stopped and looked back. The theater was different now; the marquee was there—*Ritz Theater*, it said—but it lay collapsed onto the sidewalk below, blocking the entrance completely. No one could go into the movie house as he had done because what had been was no longer there. The neon bulbs were dark and broken, as was the building itself. It was neglected and decaying just like the surrounding ones. Nothing remained of how it had looked moments earlier.

This is a dream. I'm lying on the beach unconscious, or I'm bobbing around in the ocean, or I'm in a hospital bed with nurses who are trying to get me to wake up. Maybe I died, and I'm in Heaven. Or maybe worse. Whatever, none of this is real.

When he passed the Sweet Shop, his mouth dropped. In the brief time he'd been at the theater, it too had completely changed. The sign dangled above the empty doorway, the second floor had fallen in, and the building sat empty and deserted like the others. The store, the jukebox, the milkshake machine, even Mr. Callahan—all those memories that had been real a moment ago—were gone.

Everything I saw was a figment of my imagination. I made it all up. But why? Why does a ghost town in Florida evoke poignant memories of my childhood in a place a thousand miles away?

It wasn't because things were good here. This place was evil; a presence—something that terrified Tom Horton—hung like a shroud over it. He had no idea how far it was to the next town, but he had to get out of Midnight Pass. Pumping his seventy-year-old legs as fast as they'd go, he came to the wrought-iron fence where the dusty street ended. He ran toward the opening that led to the beach but found it blocked by a spiked gate that hadn't been there when he walked through the archway an hour ago. He grabbed the bars with both hands and shook them violently, but the gate wouldn't budge.

"Hey, Tommy. You can't leave. Patti's waiting for you back at the Sweet Shop."

Startled, he turned to see Mr. Callahan and the girl Linda from the theater standing behind him. They weren't there a moment ago, and he realized that he'd crossed a line somehow—a line between today and yesterday, between reality and insanity, between everything he ever believed was real and what awaited him back in Midnight Pass.

As the two figures walked steadily toward him, he realized something else. He would never go back. Whatever was happening here, it was the end for him. He fell to his knees, held his head in his hands and cried.

CHAPTER THREE

Summer 2001
Naples, Florida

"Where are you going?" Donnie Southard's mother asked as her son reached for her car keys.

"Just down to the glades. No place in particular."

"Last time you and Will went to the Everglades, you were gone for hours, and it worried me sick. I heard that a few weeks ago, some folks pulled off the highway to have a picnic lunch. They got too close to the water, and an alligator dragged their little girl into the swamp. They never found that poor child."

Donnie and Will glanced at each other and smirked. "Geez, Mom, we're sixteen years old. I think we're smart enough not to get eaten by a gator."

"Everybody talks about how dangerous it is. If the car broke down or you had a flat, you could be in serious trouble."

Donnie's friend Will Norris tried to ease her fears. "My family's been here two years, Mrs. Southard. My dad and I have been out in the glades a lot. It seems a lot scarier than it is. We'll be fine."

Warren Southard, Donnie's father, was an administrative assistant at the Ten Thousand Islands National Wildlife Refuge near Naples. After relocating from Georgia five months ago, the family had worked to cultivate friendships among the people who lived around them. Will's family was one of those, he and Donnie went to the same school, and their parents had become friends.

This had been the fourth time Donnie's father had been transferred, and the boy had resisted the move, complaining about having to make friends all over again. In the weeks after their arrival in Naples, he'd locked himself in his room, playing video games every moment he wasn't in school, and Donnie's parents were pleased when he met Will, whose dad was an airline pilot. Nowadays the boys spent a lot of time together, especially on weekends like this one.

As Donnie pocketed his cellphone, his mother said, "I want to know the latest you'll be home. If I don't, I'll worry all afternoon. How about you be back by three?"

They negotiated for four, and as they left, she said, "Be careful, boys. And take care of my car!"

She would never see Donnie or Will again.

———

Despite what they'd told Donnie's mom, the boys knew exactly where they were going. In history class, they'd learned about the strongest storm ever to hit the Americas—the Labor Day Hurricane of 1935 that brought death and devastation to Florida's west coast. They'd also learned about the town that suffered the most—a small coastal village wiped off the map, its citizens annihilated in one awful afternoon. That town, a ghostly shell today, was called Midnight Pass. After that history lesson, Donnie and Will wanted to go check it out.

No longer on the maps, they had to search the internet to find where the town was situated and how to get there. The roadway that once led to Midnight Pass had been abandoned for decades, and that meant the boys might face hours of hiking, time they didn't have. Their plan was to play it by ear, get as close as they could, and hope it was a short trek the rest of the way in.

Wondering if it might be easier to get there by boat, they stopped at a place called Captain Jack's in Everglades City to check out the cost of renting an airboat. Between them, they had almost a hundred dollars, but that wasn't nearly enough. The fee was three hundred an hour, driver included, and it would take at least two hours to get there, check the place out, and come back. Donnie's mother's Malibu was their only choice.

They'd pilfered a couple of beers each from the garage refrigerator at Will's house, and after a quick stop at a convenience store for sandwiches and chips, they drove east out of Everglades City on Plantation Parkway. After passing through a new housing addition, they came to a roadblock—a highway department barricade. "ROAD CLOSED. NO ACCESS."

"We'd better leave the car here," Will said, but Donnie thought they could get further down, since GPS showed they were still three miles from Midnight Pass. He maneuvered the Chevy around the sign and onto a once-blacktopped road that had not seen maintenance in a very long time. Donnie swerved first right, then left to avoid chunks of asphalt that littered the pavement. A mile along, the asphalt played out, and the road became a grassy trail that jutted like a finger through the swamp.

"We shouldn't go any further," Will said. "The pathway's barely wider than the car. If it gets any narrower, we'll end up in the water. And if we keep going, we'll have to back up to get out. It's too dangerous."

Calling Will a pussy, Donnie eased the car forward

onto the narrow spit of grassy roadway. They passed by tall mangroves jutting out of the water on both sides, and they'd gotten maybe half a mile when they could go no further. Ahead of them the roadway had eroded on one side, leaving only a narrow strip of dry ground. They could go on, but they'd be walking from here, and as Will had feared, once they returned, the first half mile of their return trip in the car would be in reverse.

Will said it was stupid to have brought the car this far, but Donnie told him to shut up. "We'll be just fine. We got here, didn't we? Backing up's the same as going forward." But Will knew better, and he knew Donnie did too. His friend was too brazen sometimes, and this could turn into a big mess. Both had had their licenses less than six months, and Will was terrified Donnie might run the car off into the swamp.

"How about we go ahead and back out now and walk in? That way your mom's car will be safe, and we'll have the hard part over with."

Donnie said he wasn't backing up just to have to walk an extra half mile when they were already here. He locked the car, and they tiptoed across the narrow piece of ground. He wondered if there might be alligators hiding in the mangrove roots just three feet away. The huge reptiles could move quickly, and both of them could be dragged into the swamp before they could run.

Fortunately nothing happened, and just around a bend, the roadway widened again. After walking for twenty minutes, Donnie spotted a fence in the distance and dark buildings that rose behind it. A shiver ran down his spine as he beheld row after row of malevolent structures. He gulped, "Here we are, I guess. Midnight Pass."

CHAPTER FOUR

Donnie wished he'd brought a jacket; in the half hour they'd been walking, ominous thunderclouds had rolled in, and a stiff northerly breeze brought a sudden drop in temperature. They could taste salt in the air, a reminder of how close they were to the water. An arched gate marked the boundary of Midnight Pass; back in the day, the road would have continued through it and into town. Like the fence, it was in poor shape now, and a welcome sign lay faded and broken on the ground.

They walked into a place that preserved the memories of one fateful day like sepia photographs in an album. A rumble of thunder rolled across the darkening skies as they walked down Main Street past ruined hulks of what had once been a thriving business district. On side streets stood houses left to collapse into a pile of debris.

Donnie walked toward a rickety two-story building to observe the sign over its entryway. Below a huge pair of painted eyeglasses were the words *Dr. Miller, Optician*. He peered through the gaping holes that had been shop windows and saw the remnants of the store—frames strewn about after the cases that held them had fallen, an exam chair still upright, and an eye chart tacked to the only wall still standing. There was something else as well, back in the gloom almost too far to see. A pile of rags—clothes, maybe?—lay on the floor. Donnie felt goosebumps rise on his arms. Was that the spot where Dr. Miller met his fate on Labor Day 1935? Had he drowned right there in his exam room when the hurricane came? Was his body still there inside the clothes he wore?

Spooked, Donnie ran back to the street, but Will wasn't there. A huge bolt of lightning shot across the sky, followed immediately by a thunderclap that shook the buildings around him. He shouted for Will, but the words were lost in the cacophony. Fog had descended upon the town, and Donnie could see only a few feet ahead. He broke into a run, stopping only when he saw a light off to his right. It seemed to be coming through the window of a building, although he knew better; there had been no electricity in this ghost town for eighty years.

As he neared it, he cried out in surprise. Not only were lights visible through the windows, he recognized the interior as a place from his past. When he was close enough to see a red, white and blue barber pole, he drew back in astonishment. Painted on the brightly lit windows were the words *Matthews Barber Shop.*

Standing in the doorway was Conley Matthews, the barber who gave him his first haircut twelve years ago. But that had been in Brigham City, Utah, where his dad worked at the wildlife refuge center. The shop couldn't possibly be in a ghost town in Florida, but there was no denying its existence, because here it stood, looking exactly as it had back then.

The proprietor waved his hand and shouted, "Donnie! Come on in before you get drenched!" Dazed and confused, Donnie realized he was standing in pouring rain. He hesitated a moment as the rational part of his brain went on high alert, and then he made a decision. He ran toward the familiar front door and darted inside.

———

By then Will had wandered off down the dirt street. On a corner two blocks ahead, he noticed something unusual—a two-story edifice with a stone facade that was not only still standing but in pristine condition. The structures around it had caved in, but somehow the hotel had been spared.

The hotel. The Juliana Hotel. Will knew what this place was even before he came close enough to read the neon sign hanging from the corner. The sign flashed each letter and then lit them all at the end, just like it had back then. Five years ago, when Will turned eleven, he'd taken a job as a paperboy to earn some money after school. He'd walk the downtown streets, delivering the evening paper to businesses.

The Juliana had stood on the corner of Main Street and Rennie Avenue for decades, serving as the town's fanciest hotel in its heyday, and as a seedy brothel later on. Since they were forbidden to go there, Will would describe to his friends the dimly lit lobby, its old couches and tables dusty and faded. "Were there whores inside?" the eager preteen boys would ask, and he'd nod, spelling out in tantalizing detail how he delivered papers up on the second floor. "Some of them would be out in the hall wearing nothing but their underwear," he'd recount as they breathlessly lapped up every word.

The Juliana was a real hotel in a real town…but not this town. It was in Davidson, North Carolina. As the rain intensified, he saw a woman wearing red lipstick and a pink bra and panties lean out of a second-floor window.

"Hey, Will! Bring the papers up here before they all get wet!"

Dazed, scared and soaked, he darted into the lobby.

That smell of stale tobacco and musty furniture, the old man sitting behind the registration desk, and the pool table over in a corner of the cavernous room were all immediately familiar. Will couldn't understand how this could be happening—it was a memory from his past, but why here in a place he'd never been? How was it the only building still in one piece in the ruined town, and who would go to the immense effort to create an exact replica of a building that meant nothing in the first place?

Will felt something brush his side—the bag he used to carry his newspapers. *How did that get there?* A deep sense of resignation and defeat swept through his body. Somehow he and his friend had done the impossible—stepped through a wormhole in time, perhaps, or maybe entered a parallel dimension. He'd seen TV shows about those things, but this was real, and it was happening to him. Sensing he was past the point of no return, he wondered why he didn't just walk away.

Because he couldn't. There was no way out. That archway that led back to their car might as well be a thousand miles away, because he wasn't going to be walking through it again. Although Will knew something was dreadfully wrong about this situation, he understood he must play out the role to conclusion and see how things ended. He walked to the staircase and plodded up to the second floor, where a bevy of femme fatales—customers of a newsboy from five years ago—waited to get their afternoon papers.

In Naples at 5:30 p.m., two frantic mothers hugged each other as they spoke with the sheriff of Monroe County. The boys were late, and neither had answered his phone in hours. "We'll have a chopper in the air shortly," the officer promised. "They'll be there in under an hour, and as soon as we have something to report, I'll be back in touch."

After two hours spent pacing, weeping and having thoughts they were afraid to say aloud, Glenna Southard's phone rang. She grabbed it and cried, "Please! Please tell me they're okay."

"The deputies located your car, Mrs. Southard."

"Thank God! Where are they?"

The veteran lawman hesitated. These conversations were best had face-to-face, but he was in Key West, his men were still looking for the missing teens, and the phone would have to do. "They haven't found the boys. They drove the car past a no-trespassing barricade and onto a grassy roadbed that's been abandoned for years. About a half mile down, the roadway became so eroded and narrow they couldn't keep going, so they left the car. My men found shoe prints in the mud; a mile or so along, the road dead-ends at an abandoned village on the coast called Midnight Pass, and it looks like that's where they went. It's a ghost town today, it was destroyed in a hurricane almost a century ago, and nobody's lived there since. The deputies are still on-site, searching to see if the boys might have gotten trapped in some wreckage. They say the place is hazardous, and you'd have to watch your step if you went exploring. Now's not the time for giving up hope, Mrs. Southard. Trust me, my men will keep looking, and I'll report back as soon as I know something."

Investigators found nothing more, and the sheriff dutifully called the grieving parents, who asked the questions no one could answer. Even if they had perished somehow, there would be bodies. Where were their children, and how could they simply disappear?

CHAPTER FIVE

August 2017

Natalie Hatcher came to Florida on a mission. A retired elementary school teacher from San Antonio, she had joined a genealogy website to learn about missing pieces of her family puzzle, and she turned up an astonishing find. Three relatives—both paternal grandparents and an uncle—died on the same day in the same place. September 3, 1935. Midnight Pass, Florida.

After a brief online investigation, she found the cause of death of those relatives and over a hundred others. A ferocious hurricane that swept up the west coast of Florida had obliterated the town and killed everyone in it. After a brief period during which bodies were collected and burned, the place had been abandoned. Finding nothing current online, she decided to take a ten-day road trip, overnighting along the way at the casino in Biloxi and reconnecting with old friends in Tampa before heading down to the Everglades.

Midnight Pass hadn't been on anybody's radar in years, so she stopped for information and directions in

Everglades City at a little pink house that housed the local museum. She saw an exhibit about the Labor Day Hurricane and read the names of her three relatives on the list of those who perished. When she asked for directions, an octogenarian docent told her which road would get her closest. She copied a town plat from 1933, saying it might come in handy to locate a specific street, and after all that help, the old docent told Natalie under no circumstances should she make the trip to Midnight Pass.

"People have gone down there and never returned," the woman said. "I've lived in these parts my whole life, and folks say the devil's at work there. There's nothing to see except streets lined with falling-down buildings abandoned almost ninety years ago. Nobody survived, and since they burned the bodies, relatives felt no reason to go back. The county closed the road, put up signs to keep people out, and left the town to rot. There's nothing there, dear, so please don't put yourself at risk by going to Midnight Pass."

"There's no proof of anything dangerous there," Natalie replied sweetly. "Nobody goes there, like you said. I have the address of my grandparents' house, and I aim to see if I can find it."

"You may end up finding way more than you expected is all I have to say," the old lady muttered. "I'm telling you, people have vanished from that cursed place. But don't listen to me. Go ahead; it's your funeral."

Natalie knew about the disappearances. One in 1988, two more in 2001, and rumors of even more, but they didn't worry her. Midnight Pass was in the Everglades, an unforgiving swamp infested with creatures and a place where carelessness could lead to peril. If you fell out of a boat or stepped too close to the water's edge or ventured off the marked trails, you could quickly find yourself in big trouble. She intended to do none of those things. She'd find the town, search for the house, and leave.

Those intentions got upended from the moment Natalie pulled up to the barricade where the highway ended. She was still three miles from her destination, and stretching before her was a grassy lane that had once been the road to Midnight Pass. *I'm in no shape to walk that far,* she thought, disappointed that she'd gotten so close without reaching the goal.

As she turned to leave, she heard a noise in the distance—the sound of a motorized vehicle growing louder by the minute. To her surprise, she saw someone coming up the old roadbed on a motorcycle outfitted with a sidecar like a prop in a 1950s B-movie. She got her first look at the driver, who wore a helmet, driving gloves and goggles, and when the person shut off the engine, dismounted and approached her, Natalie's heart began beating hard and fast. Not only had the cycle and sidecar triggered a memory, she'd recognize that saunter anywhere.

Marsha? Could it be? Is it possibly true?

The helmet came off, and gray-blond hair cascaded out. Natalie ran to her sister's side, hugged her close and said, "Marsha! I thought…well, you know. We just never heard anything. We thought…oh my God, girl, we thought you died, and here you are after so many years, still riding that crazy motorcycle you owned! What on earth…how can you be here?"

It was a bizarre reunion in the Florida Everglades. As a high school senior in 1967, Natalie's sister, Marsha, had ridden an old sidecar motorcycle from San Antonio to attend a counterculture festival in San Francisco led by Timothy Leary. Once there, she joined thousands of other hippies who followed Leary's advice to "turn on, tune in and drop out." She never came home, and her family had had no word in years.

"I just can't believe my eyes! I just want to stand here and hug you forever. My word, Marsha, what you put Mom and Dad through, and now you turn up after all these years. Where have you been? How did you get here?"

Marsha broke the hug and laughed. "It's a long story, but I'll explain. Come on, sis. Hop in, and let's go to town." Natalie wedged her ample body into the sidecar, and they raced away down the narrow roadbed. Soon they reached the iron fence that encircled Midnight Pass, careened through the archway, and screeched to a halt on Main Street.

"My, this is a desolate place," Natalie said as she extricated herself from the car and voiced the doubts she'd begun having. "Hey, sis, how is it you happen to be here on the day I came to visit? Surely you don't live here. How did you know I'd be out there on the road?"

No one answered because Natalie was alone.

The day had been bright and cloudless, but now dark clouds rolled in, and a cool breeze stirred the dust in the street where Natalie stood next to the ancient motorcycle. One- and two-story buildings in varying stages of disrepair lay on both sides, standing like ruined megaliths that jutted into the low-hanging clouds. This was a sad place—a place of loss and grief and words left unsaid.

Addled, she looked this way and that before giving up on Marsha. She couldn't explain any of this, but still it was a relief to see her alive and well after so many years. Maybe she'd be back before Natalie left. Maybe she was playing some kind of joke.

Primed for her mission, Natalie took the map from her pocket and began walking to the street where her grandfather had lived. Ash Street lay one block down and two over. With such utter devastation and no street signs, she'd never have found it without the map. She dodged debris and stacks of lumber, carefully noted her location as she moved along, and finally came to the right block. 300 Ash was on her left, so her grandfather's house—314 Ash—should be five or six houses down the block, and to her astonishment, it was easy to spot. Somehow it had weathered the hurricane that had destroyed everything else, and it was impossible to miss—a neat bungalow, white with green shutters, tucked behind a picket fence and sandwiched between a block of dark, ruined houses.

An enormous bolt of lightning split the sky, followed by a powerful thunderclap and the first drops of rain from the ominous clouds. Approaching the fence, Natalie felt the hairs rise on her neck as fear gripped her; she remembered the old docent's warning, but she told herself there was an explanation for the aberration that stood before her. She was in an abandoned town. Her sister had gone somewhere but was still close, and this had once been her grandfather's house. All should be well, except that none of this made sense.

In a town where everything was hued in varying shades of black and gray, Grandfather's yard was bright green and freshly mowed. Jonquils and daisies blossomed in a little garden, and there were fresh red tomatoes on a vine that weaved through a wooden trellis. Every dwelling, every business in Midnight Pass was dark except 314 Ash Street, where lights in the windows glowed with warmth. She jumped in fright as the door opened, and a man stepped onto the porch.

That was the moment Natalie Hatcher realized it was too late to heed the old lady's warning. Midnight Pass wasn't a godforsaken, vacant town. It had inhabitants. One of them—her grandfather—was coming toward her, arms outstretched and with a big grin on his grizzled face. She'd never met him, of course, but she'd seen pictures. There was no mistaking who he was, and there was also no doubt he'd died in 1935 in this house. When her sister, Marsha, came through the door and down the walk, Natalie understood. Marsha was dead too. She'd been dead all those years, just like everyone thought.

Feeling light-headed, Natalie reached for the fencepost, missed and collapsed to the ground in a dead faint.

When Natalie failed to return to San Antonio, concerned friends reported her missing. The people she visited in Tampa said she had been on the way to Midnight Pass, where her relatives had perished in the Labor Day Hurricane. At the request of Monroe County authorities, the Everglades City chief of police sent a deputy to look around. He found Natalie's locked car at the barricade where the old highway to Midnight Pass ended. There was no sign of foul play and no indication of where she went. Since Everglades City was in a different county and outside the deputy's jurisdiction, he didn't go into the abandoned town itself. Monroe County deputies would arrive a few days later, find no clues, leave and file Natalie Hatcher's case away.

CHAPTER SIX

Two weeks ago

Grant Stark and Shannon Black were the most recent ones. Sheriff's investigators would find Grant's Subaru Outback parked at the barricade that blocked off the old road; within a few days they'd make a connection to a 2017 case where a woman's car was found in the same place, and another from 2001 involving a Chevrolet abandoned a little further along the roadway by two teenaged boys. In each case the people were never seen again.

Grant and Shannon, who lived together in Tampa, were firefighters and weekend treasure hunters who combed the beaches with metal detectors. Over time they'd discovered their hobby wasn't just fun but lucrative as well. They'd found rings and other jewelry, cellphones and coins, including a Spanish one dated in the sixteen hundreds. In just over a year, they'd made over a thousand dollars selling the trash and treasures they turned up, which covered expenses and made the hunts exciting.

Always on the lookout for beaches tucked away and forgotten by other amateur detectors, Shannon learned about the tragedy at Midnight Pass that left the town empty, the pier in ruins, and the site left to the elements. In 1935 there had been a beach, and they hoped after all the years it might yield some surprises. They left after work on Friday, spent the first night camping on the beach at Bonita Springs, and arrived at the barricaded roadway around ten on Saturday morning. Seasoned hikers, they donned backpacks and set off down the grassy roadbed toward the ghost town. When they came to the wrought-iron spike fence and archway, they saw the desolate rows of buildings in what was once a business district.

"Wow," Shannon said. "This is the creepiest place I've ever been. When we choose our campsite, it'd better be far away from here!"

They spent an hour poking around the ruins, finding a few surprises among the debris. An old Ford sign lay in the street next to a building that once had huge front windows. Two cars—now old, but once brand-new 1935 models—sat in the windows, exactly where they'd been the moment the hurricane had destroyed the dealership. Next door was Woolworth's five-and-ten; curious, Grant ducked under part of the roof that hung precipitously over the sidewalk and peeked inside. Row after row of shelves lay in ruins, the merchandise strewn about everywhere. In the ensuing years it seemed nobody had shoplifted because no living soul remained.

Around noon they found another gated archway—one that led to the Gulf—scaled a large dune and walked out onto a dirty, unkempt beach. Shannon commented that it seemed perfect; it looked as though no one had set foot on it in a long time. Unnerved by the spooky old town, she found a place to pitch a tent where the tall dune shielded the ruins of Midnight Pass from the beach. They dropped their gear and began sweeping the sand with metal detectors.

In addition to pop-tops and metal cans that had washed ashore and been buried, Grant and Shannon found several coins dating prior to the 1935 storm, a gold ring with what might be a semiprecious stone, and a silver flask with a screw top that was engraved *Henry S. Butler, 1899*, likely a keepsake that had been lost at sea.

They clinked wineglasses as the sun dropped below the horizon, and ate hot dogs and marshmallows cooked over a campfire. They talked and read on their Kindles until ten, but not long after they'd crawled into their sleeping bags, he said, "Shannon, do you hear music?"

She did—the sound of a rowdy band playing Willie's "One Toke Over the Line." They also heard distant laughter and conversation, and she sat up and looked outside. "I don't see any running lights, but it must be coming from a boat."

He crawled out of the tent, stood and pointed. "It's coming from the town."

"But that's not possible."

They crept up the tall sand dune and looked past the fence into the little town a hundred yards away. Every building was dark…except one, a brightly lit, two-story wooden structure facing the beach. Some of the patrons had spilled out into the street, the ones whose voices they heard.

"That's Cooter's Roadhouse!" he whispered. "My fraternity brothers and I went there every weekend when I was at Florida State. But how…what the hell is it doing here? How did all those people get here?"

She said, "It's some kind of vision. The building isn't there, and neither are they. It's not Cooter's Roadhouse either. It's a place called Skeeter's, just off campus at Auburn. I've been there too, but I haven't been to your place. None of this is real, Grant. Somehow we're seeing a mirage or something. We both know that place wasn't there when we walked through the town a few hours ago. Describe to me what it looks like."

He told her the building was painted white with a row of American flags hanging from the railing of a second-floor porch, and a Miller Lite sign flashed on and off in the window to the right of the entryway.

Then it was Shannon's turn. The building was red, not white. It had no upstairs porch, no Miller Lite sign, and along the top of the building the name SKEETER'S flashed in white neon, one letter at a time, then all at once. "We're seeing two different things," she said, grabbing his hand tightly. "I don't get it, but that's what's going on, and it's terrifying. We have to get out of here, right now."

He looked at her in surprise. "What are you talking about? That place isn't scary; it's just the opposite. I'm wishing I could go up there and have a beer with those people."

"Oh God, Grant, don't tell me that! This is like some weird parallel universe or something. We're seeing two different things in the same place. If we both went, what would happen? Would each of us be transported to the place we're seeing? Would we be able to get back?"

Grant accused her of overanalyzing. "This isn't some time warp or rip in the fabric of the universe," he said. "There has to be a logical explanation for it. I don't remember looking at the buildings on the exact block where the roadhouse is, so maybe it was there all along. Maybe somebody opened up a bar in an abandoned town, and at night the locals show up. I'm thinking it looks like fun."

"Just explain how they get here. We saw what used to be the pier. It's nothing but a pile of logs, just like everything in Midnight Pass is nothing but a pile of lumber. They don't come by boat, and they don't walk three miles down that roadway we hiked. I'm telling you, the place right there in front of us—Cooter's Roadhouse for you and Skeeter's for me—isn't real because it can't be. If we…if *you* walked up there…you have no idea what would happen. That place is in some kind of time warp or something, and we have to get out of here, now!"

They stood, and Shannon began gathering their gear. "Grant, help me take down the tent," she said, but he didn't answer. When she looked around, she cried out in horror. "Grant! Grant, don't do it! Come back!"

Paying no attention to her cries, he reached the top of the sand dune and disappeared on the other side. Sobbing, she ran to it, climbed up and watched as he passed through the gateway and into the town. Things at the saloon were as they'd been—music, boisterous laughter, people in the street and the neon letters blazing—and as he approached the merriment, she wondered if in his mind he was at Cooter's Roadhouse. A man handed him a beer, clapped a hand on Grant's back, and a moment later the lights went out. Literally. One second the place was filled with sound and light—the next, everything went dark.

The building lay in ruins, just like every other in Midnight Pass. None of what she'd seen existed now. Perhaps it never had. But if this was a dream…or a nightmare…when would she awaken? And would Grant be with her?

Too scared to go into the town and look for him, she walked back and sat on the sand beside their tent. As the hours passed, she knew this was no dream. She was living it in real time. Finally dawn broke, and it was time to go. The only way back was through the town, so that was what she had to do. At least it wasn't dark now. Screw the tent, Grant's pack and equipment and her own. In a daze, she stumbled over the dune and into the town. She cast a glance at the desolate block where Skeeter's bar had appeared, and trudged on to Main Street, forcing herself to keep going, one foot in front of the other.

"Shannon, over here!"

"Grant!" she screamed. "You're alive! Where are

you?" She looked all around her but saw no other living thing.

She dropped to her knees, sobbing, "Don't do this to me. Are you alive? Please, Grant. Please don't leave me here!"

"It's okay," he replied, coming up the street behind her. "Everything's fine."

Shannon leapt up and ran to hug him. "Oh God, thank you! I was so worried…" She put a hand on his face but drew back. "You're so cold! What happened…"

His face was drawn, his lips a thin line as he replied, "So much has happened. You should have come with me last night. It would have made things easier."

"Easier? What are you talking about? Let's get out of here!"

She resisted as he gripped her arm with his cold fist. "Remember when you said it wasn't real, that we were seeing two different things in the same place? Well, you were right about that. When I walked up to Cooter's last night, I ran into my fraternity brothers from back then. Somebody handed me a beer and welcomed me."

"I…I saw that. It happened just before everything went dark."

"Just before I learned the truth. You thought this might be a time warp or a parallel universe, but you were wrong. I said it might be real…and it is, but not here and not now. Cooter's Roadhouse existed once, and it exists today, here in Midnight Pass, with the same people and the same music and the same beer, for as long as I allow it to exist."

Releasing her, he turned to look at the collapsed buildings. Shannon said, "I'm not following. Are you saying what you experienced last night was only in your imagination? If that's true, how come I saw a bar from my college days too?"

"You don't understand," he said, turning to face her

as she began screaming. His voice was deep, his dark eyes a well of inky blackness, and she looked into a face that was no longer Grant Stark's. Instead, she beheld something more malevolent—more evil—than she could have conjured up in her worst nightmares.

"No one understands because Midnight Pass isn't what anyone thinks. It's a town a hurricane wiped clean, which created a canvas to allow me to work my craftsmanship. It changes as I will it to change. It is whatever I want it to be."

PART TWO

THE TOWN

CHAPTER SEVEN

Landry Drake and Cate Adams awoke to the whirring of the coffee grinder. "Look out there. Isn't it beautiful?" she said, gazing out the sliding glass doors that opened onto their second-story patio. Landry rose on one elbow and gazed at the calm azure waters fifty feet away. The sliding glass doors had been left open to let the night breezes sweep through their condo. It was a luxury they didn't have in the stifling humidity of their hometown, New Orleans.

He padded into the kitchen, brought two coffees out to the patio, and they sat in bathrobes, watching Siesta Key Beach come alive. At eight thirty on a Saturday, there were already joggers, bicyclers, dog walkers and tourists out and about, and the parking spaces along Avenida Messina, the street that ran alongside their building and dead-ended at the beach, had already been claimed by rental cars and golf carts.

"I could live here." Cate sighed. "Do you think Henri would go for relocating the Paranormal Network to Siesta Key?"

Landry's silenced phone vibrated on the glass-topped table. He laughed as he saw Henri Duchamp's name, said, "Speak of the devil," and switched on the speaker. "Good morning, Henri. How are things in the Big Easy?"

"Excellent. I hope I didn't wake you, but something odd's going on not far from you that might be worth a look. Two people have gone missing south of you near a place called Everglades City. It's about two hours from where you are now."

"Missing persons? Maybe you're getting senile, but I do paranormal stuff, remember? Not police work."

"*Senile?* Respect your elders, you young pup. I'm not yet fifty."

The close relationship among these three had brought them together as business partners. Landry Drake had become regionally well known as a paranormal investigator for a New Orleans TV station, and his girlfriend, Cate Adams, managed her father's successful psychiatric practice in Galveston, Texas. As head of the Louisiana Society for the Paranormal, Henri often aided Landry in background research for supernatural cases he investigated, and they had become fast friends.

They could not have been more different in background and personality. Henri, sophisticated and genteel at age forty-nine, sported a goatee and horn-rimmed glasses, wore a coat and tie every day, and in every way resembled the academic he was. Landry and Cate, at thirty-two and twenty-nine respectively, were less restrained. Those differences served them well when they created a partnership called the Paranormal Network, which was headquartered in one of two adjacent and quite haunted buildings on Toulouse Street in the French Quarter that Henri owned. Cate served as office manager, Henri handled research and vetted story ideas, and Landry was the on-air personality, which served to make his face familiar to viewers everywhere he went.

Now in its second year of operation, millions tuned in to the cable network to watch shows, interviews and learn about supernatural and unexplained phenomena. In recent months the most popular shows were episodes of Landry's original series *Mysterious America.*

Constantly on the lookout for new material, Landry and Henri considered each of dozens of supernatural sightings, reports and suggestions from viewers, most of which turned out to be hoaxes or unverifiable subjects. A few, including one from Savannah that ended up becoming a *Mysterious America* episode called "Serpent," were truly enigmas and kept viewers on edge as the stories unfolded.

Because so few leads ended up as possibilities, Landry had questioned Henri's suggesting a missing persons report. Even so, he knew Henri had a valid reason, because he was very good at ferreting out leads.

"Give me a break," Henri quipped, saying he'd seen the brief news item on a website he followed that focused on oddities, paranormal events and unexplained phenomena. "Another Disappearance at Midnight Pass" was the headline that had caught Henri's attention. Over the past thirty years, six persons had vanished near a ghost town on the southwest Florida coast called Midnight Pass.

On Labor Day weekend in 1935, a deadly hurricane struck the coastal village, bringing tidal waves, gale-force winds and eleven inches of rain in two hours. The storm took a terrible toll on property and persons. Every single person in the town—one hundred and sixty-two citizens of Midnight Pass—perished that afternoon. Since that day, the town had lain abandoned, its dirt streets lined with decaying buildings and homes. No one ever moved back, and people who lived in the area lost interest, given its remote location in the Everglades at the end of an unkept dirt road. Even those passing by sea would notice only a rotting pier, a dirty beach and tall sand dunes, behind which the ruined town lay hidden.

"Six people disappeared in thirty years," Landry mused. "In the Everglades, no less, where there are man-eating alligators, twelve-foot snakes and who knows what else. I have to say it sounds logical to me, but I'm sure you have more to reveal, so let's have it." Henri's penchant for disbursing interesting facts bit by bit irritated Landry at times, although he was a master at spinning a tantalizing tale.

"I found information posted by people in Everglades City, which is the closest town to Midnight Pass. They talk about how the lost souls are trapped there for eternity, doomed to inhabit the town forever. The few who've actually gone there reported eerie sensations, spooky sounds and something else that's really strange.

"Today the town consists of block after block of ruined structures that collapsed in part or in full decades ago, but three people who went there claim to have seen buildings with electricity and freshly painted exteriors, standing like new amidst rotting hulks on both sides. The three people weren't together, their visits happened over months or years, and each one saw a different building. Different blocks and different storefronts, all ruined except for one. And each time it was a building they recalled from their pasts. Something in a memory. I found that intriguing."

Ordinarily the skeptic, Henri seemed captivated by a tale Landry didn't think merited attention. "I'm on vacation," he said. "We're doing the pina colada, lunch in the little village, watch the sunset next to a beach bonfire kind of thing. I know you don't understand the concept, but I'm not interested in interrupting all that to rent a car and drive two hours for some unfounded mystery."

"An off-road vehicle. Be sure you get something like a Jeep that can go off road. From what I've read, the old highway to Midnight Pass hasn't been maintained since

1935. Today it's virtually impassable. Oh, and the mystery's not unfounded at all. Those people really did disappear, never to be heard from again."

Cate smiled as she listened to their banter and wondered who would ultimately prevail. "Hello?" Landry said. "Did you miss the part about me not being interested?"

Henri continued, "You have three days of vacation remaining. If you lie around on the beach all day, you'll end up with a nasty sunburn. Get up tomorrow morning, drive down to Everglades City, and talk to people. If you can get to Midnight Pass, even better. If you leave by sunrise, you can be back by lunchtime."

"Henri, listen to me. People on vacation don't get up at sunrise and drive two hours to see an abandoned town. They lie in bed and drink coffee on the patio, except when annoying phone calls interrupt their reverie. Are you getting my drift?"

Silent until now, Cate raised her hand and whispered, "I vote with Henri." Landry's eyes widened, and he blurted, "Are you kidding?" which prompted Henri to ask what was going on. As equal partners, they'd agreed from the start that any new project required unanimous consent. That allowed Landry's exuberance to be tempered by Henri's penchant for painstaking research and Cate's even-keel business mind. Checking out a potential project involved money, and she held tight to the Paranormal Network's purse strings.

"Cate votes to go to Midnight Pass," he told Henri, and she explained that to visit the Everglades would take only a few hours out of their remaining days, and the only expenses would be gas and a rented Jeep. "Since we're here, why not take a look?" Landry gave in and made it unanimous.

The sun hadn't yet risen when, coffees in hand, they headed toward Siesta Key's south bridge in their newly rented four-wheel-drive Wrangler. They waited in line a few minutes while the Stickney Point drawbridge opened for a passing yacht, then crossed into Sarasota and headed south on Interstate 75. At Naples they left the highway and continued south on smaller roads that allowed occasional glimpses of the Gulf. By eight they were in Everglades City, having breakfast at the Island Café, and then it was off to the most imposing building in the tiny community—city hall.

The police chief, an affable man in his fifties named Hawkins, ushered them into his cramped office. He'd seen Landry's episode called "Serpent," called himself a rabid fan, and when Landry explained they'd come to check out a possible story, the chief nodded.

"Midnight Pass, right? You're here about the couple who disappeared recently."

"Right. It may be nothing…"

"I thought that might be it, although technically you've come to the wrong place. We're the southernmost incorporated town in Collier County. If you go just a few miles south from here, you're in Monroe County. Problem with that is that ninety-nine percent of Monroe's population lives on the Florida Keys. Hardly anyone lives in the Everglades, and there's no law enforcement presence anywhere in Monroe County on the west side of Florida. Seems odd that my office is eleven miles from Midnight Pass, but I have no jurisdiction. Neither does the Collier County Sheriff's Department in Naples."

"So you can't tell us anything about those people who disappeared two weeks ago?" Cate asked.

Chief Hawkins smiled. "That's not what I said. In exchange for an autograph when we're done, I'd be happy to tell you everything I know, but I should begin with the mysteries surrounding the town itself."

CHAPTER EIGHT

"There are valid reasons why Midnight Pass has been called the most haunted town in Florida. There are all kinds of stories about supernatural events and strange sightings. My grandpa used to say that ignorant people out in the glades blamed 'haints' for things they didn't understand, but intelligent folks from all walks of life have reported strange happenings there. I've felt things there myself.

"I grew up ten miles north of here in Copeland, and the biggest event to ever take place in these parts was the Labor Day Hurricane in 1935. It's still the most intense storm ever to make landfall in the western hemisphere, and it killed hundreds of people all along the coast. Midnight Pass suffered the worst human toll per capita—every living soul in that little town died, a hundred and sixty-two of them. And even though their relatives refused to go back to the town, they passed down stories that got more outlandish with every retelling, like those things sometimes do.

"It's a fact that once the storm passed, the fierce tropical heat returned. When rescue workers finally made it down to Midnight Pass, they found dead bodies everywhere—lying in the streets, in collapsed houses and buildings—wherever the wind and waves caught up with them. The stench of death was overpowering; corpses had swelled up and burst like balloons, spewing blood and guts everywhere. The health department sent front-end loaders so workers could pick up bodies without having to handle them. They piled the cadavers in a huge stack and set them on fire."

"My God," Landry said. "With a history like that, I can see how the town has a reputation for being haunted."

"To be honest, the place scares me. Stuff goes on there, and I have no desire to go back. The 1935 storm wasn't the first; a storm in 1920 killed fifty. The survivors rebuilt their homes and businesses, but nobody new moved there, which is why the population was only 162 by 1935. Today it's zero…or so most people believe. Others claim something lives there. There are stories about a fearsome creature that roams the Everglades, killing anyone unlucky enough to be out in the swamps after dark. Personally I don't believe in swamp monsters, but some of the other stories are a hell of a lot more believable…as long as you're willing to accept the supernatural exists.

"Old-timers claim it's a cursed place—a place the devil chose to work his pleasures. Satan rode the hurricane into town that day and slaughtered every living soul. He left no survivors—not even a child. Those bloated bodies, ruined buildings and the stench of death that exists to this day—that's why people say Midnight Pass isn't in Florida…or even in America. It's in Hell.

"According to legend, after the storm, rescuers working in the night heard people's cries coming from inside their destroyed houses. When they searched, they found only corpses, even though the wailing could still be heard in other places around town. Some workers described eerie sensations, like someone was standing behind them or calling their name, but no one was there. Some got so spooked they swore they'd never set foot there again. Even the rescue dogs acted strangely, at times they'd get close to locating a body, but then they'd recoil in fright and run away howling. Once the recovery efforts ended, nobody ever went back. The road from Everglades City deteriorated to the point it's nothing more than a trail today. As the years went by, most people forgot about Midnight Pass, thank God."

Landry asked where the bodies had been buried, but the officer had no idea. Since they'd had heavy equipment, he thought they might have dug a mass grave.

Cate said, "Do you believe in the paranormal?"

"Not officially, but there are things that defy explanation in Midnight Pass. It's not my town—it's not even in my county. I hope I never set foot in that place again. You shouldn't go either—nobody should."

"You went before, you say. Why was that?"

"It was years ago, back when I was in high school. A couple of friends and I drove around the barricade, and when we couldn't get any farther, we walked on into town. The day had been sunny, but when we got there, storm clouds and a stiff breeze came out of nowhere in seconds. I felt anxious, like a weight was pushing on my chest. We were going to split up and look around, but the other guys sensed something too. 'Let's stick together,' I remember one saying. 'This place is eerie as hell.' And we did. We poked around and saw nothing but a bunch of fallen-down buildings. There was nobody there, but I got a very bad feeling about the place. I can't explain it."

Landry asked, "So you're certain it's haunted?"

"I'm certain of this—things aren't right there. When you consider what the rescue workers heard at night, then the tales about random people disappearing and the stories from fishermen who tied up to the old pier at Midnight Pass and skedaddled when they saw and felt things they couldn't explain, you get a lot of stuff that isn't right. I figure a lot more people have disappeared since 1935 than we're aware of." He enumerated those who'd been reported missing over the past thirty years—a fisherman caught in a storm, two teenagers from Naples, a retired schoolteacher and the couple who vanished two weeks ago.

"The investigators found the most recent couple's vehicle parked and locked up at the barrier and located their campsite on the beach. For some reason, they left their backpacks right in the middle of Main Street in Midnight Pass. These were young, fit individuals accustomed to camping and hiking, and like the others, they vanished without a trace."

"Any theories as to what happened to them?" Cate asked.

"It may sound bizarre, but since you asked, my personal opinion is that the devil's still doing his work in that cursed town."

Even Landry found that a little hard to accept. "With all respect," he said, "you're basing your opinion on an odd feeling you had a long time ago and a bunch of stories even you admitted get wilder with each retelling. I'm looking for substance. I believe in the paranormal, and I've spent years hunting ghosts, but I haven't heard anything about what happened in Midnight Pass that's beyond the realm of explanation."

"I understand why you're skeptical. You have to have experienced it yourself to believe it. The eerie sensations, the feeling that you're not alone—it all adds up. On second thought, maybe you should go down to Midnight Pass. You're a paranormal investigator; you'll see what I'm talking about."

Landry asked if the county sheriff might be able to add more to the story, and the chief shook his head. "I don't know a lot about the place, but I know more than either sheriff. Like I said earlier, Midnight Pass is in Monroe

County, which means it's four hours from Key West, the county seat. East Naples, our county seat, is way closer, but Charlie Veck—he's the sheriff of Collier County—is only in his thirties. I doubt he ever heard of Midnight Pass until that couple disappeared a few days back. The sheriff down in Key West has never seen this end of Monroe County, I'd bet. There's nobody to protect—no towns, no people, nothing but the Everglades."

"Since we're here, it makes sense for us to check it out," Cate said. "Maybe we'll feel things like you did, Chief. At the least we can see what the town looks like today."

Chief Hawkins said, "You all want to go down there, be my guest. I'll give you directions. Just remember I gave you fair warning."

CHAPTER NINE

In their four-wheel-drive Wrangler, Landry easily navigated around the barricade and down the roadbed that had once been the highway to Midnight Pass. Even though in places the swamp had claimed part of the roadway, their vehicle handled the narrow lane easily, and soon they came to the fence and the desolate ghost town. They parked and walked through the archway that led to Main Street.

"It's like a Hollywood set preserved in time," Cate commented, pausing to take in the surreal scene. "Do you feel the sadness and grief and memories? It's as if they've become a part of the fabric of this place. It's almost overpowering."

He didn't feel anything, which surprised neither of them, since Cate had always been the sensitive, perceptive one. During seances and when searching old houses, Landry had encountered the supernatural—eerie things impossible to explain—but his partners Henri and Cate had more sensory experiences than he because, surprisingly, they were more attuned to the paranormal than the ghost hunter himself.

As far as the eye could see, buildings in shambles lined both sides of the street and the side roads. Landry wondered where the bodies had been buried after the mass cremation. He walked to a corner building, one of the few made of brick, and looked through an empty window frame. This had been a bank; its old-fashioned wooden teller windows still stood in a row along one side of a rectangular lobby. An enormous safe door, partially blocked by collapsed ceiling beams, occupied the back wall. Landry imagined a bank vice president rushing to close the massive round door as the hurricane approached. If it could be opened today, its contents might be a fascinating time capsule of currency, coins and records from the Great Depression. He considered going inside to look around but decided against it when he noticed the vaulted ceiling had partially collapsed, sending furniture from second-story offices crashing to the lobby floor below. It was too dangerous to go inside; part of the wall would have to come down before someone could get to that vault door.

For an hour Landry and Cate explored the streets, walking block by block past what had been stores, service stations, restaurants and homes. As the only living souls in Midnight Pass, they felt as though they were intruders in some macabre ghost story. The storm had done a horrific job—not a single building remained untouched, although some second-story facades still stood precariously. Signage lay strewn about—Sunoco, Chrysler, Woolworth—poignant testimony that people once called this spooky village home. Today the town was a shrine to massive destruction, left to the mercy of the elements by heirs who never returned to claim their property or their dead.

They came to what had obviously been the town square—a piece of ground fronted on four sides by two-story buildings. A ruined gazebo stood in the center next to an enormous pile of blackened, burnt wood. Landry walked over to it and said, "I'll bet this is the place where they burned the bodies of the victims."

Cate shrugged off a chill that ran down her spine. She took his hand as they stood in silence, contemplating the horrors the rescue team must have felt as they went about their grisly task. "That pile of lumber is still stacked up," she pointed out. "After the…the cremation of all those people, they would have used a tractor or something to move the bodies to a burial place, right? So shouldn't that pile of burnt timber be a lot flatter?"

"Are you thinking they didn't bury the bodies? Maybe they burned them and just left them there?"

When she didn't reply, he turned to her and saw tears rolling down her cheeks. "I hope not," she whispered. "They perished in such an awful way. Surely the workers didn't make them suffer the disgrace of being abandoned on a makeshift trash heap. Let's get out of here, Landry. This place is starting to get to me." Without further comment, they abandoned the ghost town and returned to civilization.

Back on the island, a walk on the beach at sunset helped clear their heads, and afterwards they walked up Avenida Messina to Siesta Key Village, a vibrant shopping and dining area. At a restaurant called Summer House recommended by some residents they met, they found a surprising change from typical beach fare, including excellent cocktails and upscale entrees. An hour later, exhausted after a hard, stressful day and a wonderful dinner, they returned to the condo and called it a day.

Some time later, Landry opened his eyes and took in a familiar scene from his past. He was a deputy sitting at his desk in the Iberia Parish Sheriff's Office, a place where he had worked fresh out of college years ago. Others were there—the sheriff, the girl who ran the front desk, another deputy who'd been his friend. A noise—frantic cries for help from outside—brought them all to their feet. Landry and the other deputy ran for the door and flew out into the town square...which suddenly wasn't the town square anymore.

The scene was surreal and dumbfounding...and devoid of anyone but the two of them. Whoever had cried for help was nowhere to be seen, and while the sheriff's office had sat on a square in New Iberia, Louisiana, Landry and his friend stood in a dirt street fronted by ruined buildings. Shivering in a bitter wind, he tried to make sense of it. He turned around and saw his boss—Sheriff Willie Barbour—standing in the doorway of his office. He yelled, "What's up out there, boys? Is anything wrong?"

Landry said to his friend, "We're in Midnight Pass, but that's impossible, isn't it? The sheriff's right over there in New Iberia. I can see him standing there, but we're in another place and time."

Hearing no response, he turned and saw his friend's face had twisted into a grotesque grimace, and his eyes gleamed a hellish red. "Things are just fine out here!" the deputy cried out to the sheriff. Then he laughed, low at first, increasing to a maniacal cackle like a banshee's cry. Landry ran toward the office, but it vanished, becoming just another decrepit structure in Midnight Pass, Florida.

He awoke in a cold sweat and slept little, as the same dream plagued him each time he slumbered. At last dawn broke; exhausted, he escaped from nightmare to daylight.

"You don't look so good," Cate commented as they sat on their patio, watching the waves sweep onto the sandy beach. "Can I get you another cup of coffee?"

"Please. I didn't sleep worth a damn. I kept dreaming about Midnight Pass." He described how the New Iberia sheriff's office appeared in a block of collapsed buildings and then disappeared. "The office was exactly as it looked when I worked there years ago, but it was transplanted to Midnight Pass somehow. During the dream, that part didn't seem odd to me. Everything was so real. What do you think it was about?"

"You're still thinking about what we saw. That visit to Midnight Pass was hard on both of us. I sensed the presence of the people who perished, and it frightened me. We have to let it go. Today's our last day here, and there are a couple of things I want to do before we leave. I'd like to visit the Ringling Museum, come back to Lido Key, look at the shops in St. Armands Circle, have lunch at a famous Cuban restaurant called Columbia, and hang out on the beach this afternoon."

"Sounds like a good plan. I agree we have to let Midnight Pass go. As spooky as the place is, I don't think there's anything to justify our spending any more time there." She agreed, and they spent their last day just as she'd planned it.

CHAPTER TEN

Two days later
New Orleans

Its streets quiet after a night of revelry, the French Quarter comes alive as the sun rises over the Mississippi River. Instead of raucous tourists and college students, the morning brings out street sweepers, garbage trucks, men hosing down sidewalks, shopkeepers standing in doorways, and residents picking up to-go coffees and beignets on their way to the office buildings on Canal and Poydras Streets.

Landry and Cate sat in the courtyard at Cajun Pride, a Toulouse Street restaurant and pub on the ground floor of the building where they worked. Most mornings they kick-started the day here with chicory coffee and a croissant. Her phone buzzed; she mouthed, *It's Caryn White*, and answered. Landry watched her lips go tight and heard her terse questions between periods of silence. Something was wrong—someone was missing—and he tensed as he wondered if it was his good friend Jack Blair. When the call ended, he could see her distress as she put a hand on his arm, took a deep breath and said, "Let's go up to the office so I can tell you and Henri at the same time. This isn't something I want to have to go through twice."

"Just tell me if it's Jack." She nodded as they climbed the narrow eighteenth-century staircase that led up to their offices and studio. In the conference room above the courtyard, she told Landry and Henri about the call from their friend Caryn, whose boyfriend had Landry's old job as senior investigative reporter for a New Orleans TV station.

"Jack's missing," she told them. "He's been on assignment and hasn't been heard from in forty-eight hours. She's filed a missing person report, but this blew me away, Landry. They found his car near Midnight Pass."

That was a shock. "How…how's that possible? We just came home…what was he doing there? Why didn't he tell us he was in the area?" His stomach churning, he stood and walked to a window. Directly across Toulouse Street was the vacant building where he had met Jack less than three years ago. Back then he had been living in a cardboard box in a recessed doorway, and he had told Landry amazing secrets about the building where Landry stood—the haunted edifice that today was their headquarters. Jack's startling revelations had provided the meat for "Die Again," an episode of Landry's popular *Bayou Hauntings* series. That nationally broadcast program had accelerated Landry's career as a television personality and paranormal investigator.

Landry had seen potential in the homeless alcoholic, given him a chance, and celebrated his victories as he became a successful investigative reporter. When Landry left to help create the Paranormal Network, Jack had been promoted to Landry's position. Although Channel Nine no longer created its own supernatural programming, Jack stayed in close touch with Cate, Henri and Landry, and they often called on him for extracurricular help. He loved the mysterious and unexplained as much as they, and his research capabilities were on par with Henri's own.

Cate continued, "He was working with their affiliate station in Naples on a human interest story about life in the Everglades—people's jobs, how tough it is living remotely, how they ride out hurricanes—that sort of thing. He and a cameraman from Naples had been staying in Everglades City. The afternoon before Jack was due to return to New Orleans, he let the cameraman go home, saying he wanted to spend his last afternoon just hanging out. No one's heard anything from him since then."

A sheriff's deputy had found his locked rental car at the barricade where the old road to Midnight Pass ended. Landry and Cate had been there too; in fact, they'd likely driven around it just one day before Jack disappeared.

His girlfriend, Caryn, had called the rental car agency at Fort Myers airport and learned the car was overdue, and the airline advised her he hadn't caught his flight home. She called the Collier County sheriff to report him missing, and an officer happened to find Jack's car. Since the location was actually in a different county, it took more than twenty-four hours for a deputy to check out the area, including the abandoned town of Midnight Pass, and report that there was no sign of the missing man.

At the end of the call, Caryn had begged for help, saying, "We all know Jack would never disappear like this. Something's really wrong—I can feel it. Please, please ask Landry to help find him."

They brainstormed; Landry and Cate had only been back from that area a couple of days; should they go right back? Given the convoluted situation involving law enforcement and jurisdiction, could they expect cooperation from the police and sheriff? Six persons had disappeared in that area over the last thirty years, and not a single clue had ever surfaced. Would anyone devote the time to help them find the latest one?

Landry suggested calling Chief Hawkins, whom he and Cate had met in Everglades City. Whatever he knew about the disappearance, his honest assessment about how much help they could expect from law enforcement would be beneficial. The police chief answered his call immediately, and as it turned out, he knew a lot, since it had been his deputy who had strayed several miles out of his jurisdiction down a dead-end road to where Jack's vehicle sat at the barricade. Hawkins had stationed officers at the scene until a sheriff's deputy from Key West arrived the next day to assume command. They had dusted for fingerprints and found only Jack's. There was no sign of foul play—the car had been locked, and Jack's phone and iPad were in the glove box. Everything pointed to Jack's having driven to the site, walked away from the car, and vanished.

Cate and Henri returned to work, leaving Landry alone in the conference room with his thoughts. He'd been so proud of Jack's accomplishments as he overcame the adversity of addiction and built a new, sober existence one small step at a time. Landry's gamble to help a homeless drunk had paid off handsomely as Jack turned his life around and became an integral part of the WCCY-TV team, giving Landry credit for having provided a helping hand every time Jack needed it most. Now that Landry had moved on—albeit just around the corner from WCCY's Royal Street studio—they continued to meet up as often as their schedules allowed. Now his friend and onetime protege was missing, and Landry was scared.

What should I do? What will help Jack the most? Is going back to Florida a waste of time? At least it would be boots on the ground where it happened...whatever that means.

He wondered if Midnight Pass was a part of this, since Jack's rental car had been abandoned at a barrier three miles away. Any number of things might have happened instead—a deranged killer; a kidnapping, but there had been no ransom call; a robbery, but Jack's phone and iPad were in the car.

Chief Ed Hawkins gave Landry his candid assessment of the situation. The only lawman likely to help Landry was Hawkins himself; they had already met; he was a self-proclaimed fan and had told them a lot about the mysteries of Midnight Pass. But his hands were tied; he had only two deputies and lacked jurisdiction. He doubted the Monroe County sheriff would expend much effort on the case, and Jack had no family or influential connections who could pull strings and move the investigation along. On that discouraging note, Landry said he'd be back in touch and disconnected.

He may not have connections, but he has me, and by God, I'll do anything I can to find him.

He walked to Cate's desk and asked her to book a flight to Fort Myers for tomorrow, saying he'd rather be on-site than fretting around here getting nothing done. "I may be looking for him all by myself, but at least I'll be doing something productive."

She flashed a smile. "I'm already on it. I knew you'd go—what else could you do? I booked two seats on Southwest's nonstop at 9:05 in the morning."

"Two seats?"

"I'm going back with you. The tragedy that happened there is beyond imagination. As eerie and forbidding as that place is, there's something that draws me to it. We haven't begun to figure out the secrets of Midnight Pass, and it looks like Jack might be part of them now. I want to be there to help, he's my friend too, and I'm really worried. They say time is critical in missing person cases. The longer it takes, the less chance of things turning out positively. We have to find him soon, and it sounds like we have more interest in solving this case than the authorities."

CHAPTER ELEVEN

Landry and Cate checked in at the Ivey House, a cozy, modern bed-and-breakfast on Buckner Avenue, one of the two primary streets in the tiny hamlet of Everglades City. From there it was an eight-mile drive to the barricade and three miles further to Midnight Pass. Finding a nice B&B in a town of less than four hundred people was a pleasant surprise, and the owners explained that tourism swelled the population throughout the year. Fishing, airboat rides, eco-tours and nature trails were some of the attractions that lured people to the southern tip of Collier County.

They'd rented another Jeep Wrangler at the Southwest Florida Regional Airport in Fort Myers, and after an early lunch at Island Café, a diner with a six-foot stuffed gator that greeted guests at the door, they stopped again at city hall to talk with Chief Hawkins. "After our conversation yesterday, I figured I might be seeing you," he said. "You knew that fellow Jack Blair pretty well, I take it."

"I *know* him," Landry said, emphasizing the present

tense. “We worked together in New Orleans, and he’s a good friend. When we came earlier, you said that people had vanished over many years, but this hasn’t happened before, right? A couple went missing recently, and now, only weeks later, Jack’s gone too. Did you go down there this time?”

“I had to because it started out as my case. Your friend and a cameraman from Naples had been filming in the area for a week. They did a lot—they toured the swamps in an airboat, interviewed fishing boat captains, the people who run the gas station, the librarian and even me. You get my drift—they spent a lot of time getting to know people around here, and most folks appreciated it. A lot of tourists who show up here think it’s a hick town populated by illiterates, and it’s nice when someone, especially a newsman doing a documentary, devotes the time and energy to finding out what makes people tick. When his girlfriend reported him missing, the search was focused around Everglades City until I found his car down at the barricade.”

“I didn’t realize you were the one who found the car. Had you and Jack discussed Midnight Pass while he was here?”

“Yeah, and I probably got him fired up to go down there and look around. I described the place and mentioned the mysteries, and he got fired up about it. He even asked for directions, and that’s what made me decide to go down to the barricade and look for him.”

“Jack’s like Landry,” Cate said with a rueful smile. “Give him something mysterious and eerie and creepy and he can’t wait to go take a look for himself, danger be damned.”

“The initial call came from—” he looked at a paper on his desk “—from a Caryn White, Mr. Blair’s girlfriend. She wanted to file a missing person report, and I told her I’d met with him several times while he was in town. We’re a tiny police force and stretched thin, so Sheriff Veck sent a couple of men from Naples to question people here in town and look for clues. I drove down to check out the barricade and found his locked rental car. He was nowhere around."

"Did you go on to Midnight Pass?"

He had, even though it was out of his jurisdiction, because it would take more than twenty-four hours for the Monroe County deputy to arrive, and time was critical in missing person cases. He had gone to Midnight Pass despite his earlier promise never to set foot in that place again, and he saw nothing but the same desolation Landry and Cate had experienced. "It was as eerie and spooky as I remembered it," he added, "but there were no clues about Mr. Blair's whereabouts. The sheriff detectives combed the town too, and we all came away empty-handed. Jack Blair vanished, just like all the others."

They thanked Chief Hawkins and headed south, going around the barricade and taking the last three miles in four-wheel drive. They walked to the square where they supposed the bodies had been cremated. As they went along, everything seemed just as it had been the last time, and there was no sign of Jack.

"We don't know if he made it this far," Cate said as they headed back to the Jeep. "There's nothing to indicate he did, so he could have gotten into trouble somewhere else. That barrier's on the edge of the swamp, and I can't imagine the creatures hiding out in there waiting to attack unwary people."

"Wherever he is, he's alive," Landry replied. "I'm certain of that, and I won't give up. He's resourceful and careful, and it looks to me like the only danger in this town is if someone ventured into one of these shaky old buildings. They could collapse at any time, but nothing indicates he came to Midnight Pass. We need to look somewhere else, not here."

Just then they discovered they weren't alone. A

young African-American man emerged from a side street, wearing khakis and a name tag that read *BUDDY ELKINS, Florida Department of Transportation*. He waved and said, "Hey, good morning! Thought I might find someone here! I guess that's your Jeep over by the gate."

"It is. Landry Drake, and this is my friend Cate. We didn't expect to find anyone here."

"I recognize you," the man said. "I've watched your TV shows, and I get why you'd want to come here. This place is crazy spooky. By the way, I'm an assistant supervisor with DOT, and my official job ends at that barricade you all went right around."

"Oh gosh, we're sorry about that..." Cate began, but he shushed her.

"Don't think a thing about it. You have the right vehicle for it, and maybe it's technically trespassing, but who cares? There's nobody here!"

"Who owns these buildings and houses today?" Landry asked, and Buddy guessed it was heirs of those who perished in 1935. "Far as I know, nobody's ever claimed ownership. Who'd want to, the shape this place is in? Like I said, there's nobody here to raise an objection to people wandering around. Just be careful, there's an awful lot of debris, and you could get hurt."

Landry said, "You said your job ends at the barricade. Do you know anything about the man whose car was found there a few days ago?"

"I only know what I heard on the news. He was a journalist from Louisiana, as I recall. I wasn't in the area then, but sometimes this place draws me in like a magnet. I can't explain why. I come down here once every month or so to check things out, be sure nobody got stranded on the road, things like that. Usually I'll walk around awhile, but when things start happening, I run like hell and get back to civilization."

"Things like what?"

"Unexplained things, I guess you'd say. When I'm here, I can't help but think about those people who died so suddenly. I don't believe in ghosts and such, but even though it draws me in somehow, this place also totally creeps me out. All these buildings are in shambles, right? But one time I looked down the street and saw a storefront from back when I was a kid in Cleveland. In between piles of lumber stood that one shop, all bright and new looking, with windowpanes and a sign and everything, exactly like the one from years back."

Exactly like my recurring dream about the sheriff's office in New Iberia, Landry thought. "What did you do?"

"I got the hell out of here. It was a while before I got the courage to return, but I never saw that building again. Had to be my mind playing tricks on me. As real as it seemed, that store was in Ohio, not Florida, and it was a long time ago. It was like some kind of flashback, but you know something funny? A part of me wishes I'd gone down the street and checked it out. It was so warm and friendly looking, and I wonder to this day if the lady who ran it would have been standing there when I walked in. Crazy, huh?"

No, not crazy. No crazier than seeing the sheriff and my old friend the deputy right here in Midnight Pass.

"Have you seen anything since?" Cate asked.

"*Seen?* No, I guess not. *Felt*, yeah. I've felt stuff every time I come here. This isn't a town you want to stay in very long. Way too much bad stuff happened here. Too many people died, and maybe their souls or something are still trapped in Midnight Pass. What do I know? I'm just a DOT worker. You're the paranormal investigator, Landry. What do you think?"

It was a question often asked, and Landry gave a canned reply. "I'm a firm believer in the paranormal, but many people use it to explain every odd or unusual event they see. There are logical answers to most so-called unexplainable occurrences. Sometimes figuring it out is easy and sometimes not. But I'd estimate ninety-nine percent of the tips we get about paranormal events are anything but."

Buddy nodded but said he'd swear on his mother's grave he saw that store from his childhood right down the street.

I know what you mean, Landry thought. *In my dreams I saw the sheriff's office from way back when...right here in Midnight Pass.*

"Some people went missing two or three weeks ago," Cate said. "A couple who'd been camping on the beach. Did you hear anything about them?"

"I heard, sure. Everybody around here heard about them. A woman disappeared a few years ago, and others before her. People start blaming the town for them disappearing, like it gobbled them up or something. Midnight Pass may be spooky and creepy, but it's not something out of a Stephen King book. The storm killed everybody, not the town."

Landry asked, "When they burned the bodies after the hurricane, did they bury them? Is there a cemetery, or did they dig a trench? We saw a big pile of burned lumber in a square a few streets over. Do you think that's where it happened?"

"Maybe. I saw that pile of boards too, but until now I never thought about it being the place they burned all those folks up. The town's surrounded by a spike fence—the one you came through to get here. Maybe there's a graveyard somewhere outside it. I've never heard tell of it, but people at the museum in Everglades City might know."

"We'll stop by and ask. One more thing—the police chief in Everglades City told us something odd. He said the old-timers claim the devil brought the storm to Midnight Pass, killed everyone and never left. He's still doing his work here today. Have you ever heard a story like that?"

"Yeah, but that's crazy talk, you know? It's legends and folklore and the like. I'll give you some advice, though. I don't think I'd be going around talking about the devil being here. You might end up regretting it. You all be careful now. I need to get to work."

"Regretting what? What do you mean by that?" Landry asked, but Buddy had walked away. He gave a wave and disappeared around a corner.

"What did he mean?" Cate wondered on the drive back. "How could we regret talking about the devil being in Midnight Pass?"

It would be days before they learned more about Buddy Elkins. By then it would be too late to turn back.

CHAPTER TWELVE

Help me, Landry! Help me!

Bathed in sweat, Landry sat bolt upright in bed and screamed, "Jack, where are you?"

Startled out of a deep sleep, Cate grabbed his arm. "You're dreaming again." His outburst—the third nocturnal awakening in as many nights since their return from Florida—had scared her the first time. By now, she'd learned he'd be asleep again in minutes. But this time was different.

"He's in trouble, Cate. He's reaching out to me the only way he can—in my dreams. Everything's so real, and he's going to die if I don't save him."

She sat up, turned on the bedside lamp, and looked at the clock. It was a quarter to six. "Why don't you tell me about it?"

He fixed two cups of coffee and took them out to their cozy third-floor patio overlooking St. Philip Street. He and Cate loved starting their mornings out here. They could see a barge lazily moving upriver on the Mississippi three blocks away, and he heard the faint sounds of Dixieland music coming from Café Du Monde over on Decatur. Even this early, they'd be serving chicory coffee and beignets to diehard revelers on the way to bed and merchants ready to start another workday.

For years, Landry had claimed he never dreamed. He knew better, he dreamed like everyone else, but he never remembered them. Now, ever since their return from Midnight Pass, he'd been plagued by them. First were the recurring sequences involving the sheriff's office that played out all one night but never again. Now there were these nightmares—frantic pleas for help from a friend in a terrifying situation.

"I'm looking down a long, dark tunnel. Everything around me is pitch black, and the only thing I can see is a tiny speck of red light at the far end. There's frigid air rushing through the passageway, and I'm shivering in the cold. Although I'm not moving, the light in the distance grows larger and larger, like it's moving toward me. Soon I can see a figure—a man dressed in white surrounded by flames that reach from his feet to his neck. His hands are outstretched, and there's a look of pure agony on his face. He's dying—he's being burned alive—and now I'm aware of voices that seem to come from all around me, rising and falling in a crescendo of awful words. But there are other sounds. Screams. Horrific wails of unimaginable pain."

Throw them on top of that pile of lumber.

Stack them as high as you can.

We'll do them all at once.

Stand back! I'm about to light it!

"The victims weren't all dead. They burned people alive that day, Cate. That's what the dream was all about. The man dressed in white is wrapped in cloth. Somehow I know that's what they did to the victims; they wrapped them to avoid touching them, and threw them on a funeral pyre. And now Jack's crying out for help. Something terrible is going to happen to him too, and I get the feeling I'm the only one who can stop it. That place at the far end of the tunnel, filled with red flames surrounding a person wrapped in white, is in Midnight Pass. We saw it. That pile of charred wood where they burned the people is the gateway to Hell."

She rose, put her arms around him, and pulled him close. "Oh my God, Landry. That's horrible. What an awful nightmare. No wonder…"

"But the awful part is that I know it's not a nightmare. I'm seeing something that happened in 1935, and Jack's telling me he's next."

"Why is he reaching out to you? What can you do?"

"That's the question, isn't it? What *can* I do? I'm not sure, but I'm beginning to think something evil inhabits Midnight Pass, and it's been there for a long time. I have this odd feeling whatever's in Midnight Pass wants me to come there, and it's using Jack as bait. Seems crazy, but I get this terrible premonition that I've pissed off the wrong person."

He slogged through the day, accomplishing nothing while racking his brain for ways to help Jack. At five, hoping to change his mood, she took him to his favorite restaurant, Muriel's, for cocktails and dinner, but all evening Landry's mind was a thousand miles away. She knew what was eating at him, but she had no way to make things better.

Although it terrified her, she knew what Landry was going to do next.

CHAPTER THIRTEEN

For the third time in eight days, Landry was in Everglades City. Despite Cate's pleas and warnings, he asked her not to come along this time because this was something he had to handle himself. Yesterday morning, after a third night with the recurring dream, he'd booked a flight to Fort Myers, and surprisingly, that action seemed to mollify the ghosts of Midnight Pass, because last night there had been no nightmare.

Today Landry drove from the airport to his first stop, a tidy pink building on Broadway in Everglades City that housed the local museum. He was pleased to find that the volunteer docent, who introduced herself as Emma Tate, was an older woman. He needed solid information about the 1935 Labor Day Hurricane, and someone Emma's age might have firsthand stories from their parents.

She recognized Landry, gushed about how much she enjoyed his documentaries, and ended up having valuable information for him. Born in 1937 on a farm outside nearby Copeland, she recalled her parents' memories of that awful Labor Day. Hearing storm warnings on the radio, they had packed up and moved inland up Highway 29 to her uncle's farm in Immokalee. After riding out the hurricane, they returned home and made repairs. It wasn't until a day or so later, when her father went to town for supplies, that he heard what had happened at Midnight Pass.

"Once he found out, he volunteered for cleanup and was assigned to the crew that gathered the bodies. You've heard that they were all cremated together?"

He nodded.

"The bodies were in rough shape, having been left out in the hot sun for several days. The description of it was so graphic my parents wouldn't tell me until I was in high school for fear it would scare the wits out of me. And it did, even all those years later. Suffice it to say, it was awful what those workers saw."

"What did they do with the bodies?"

"They laid out white sheets on the ground next to each one and just rolled them up. The…the bad stuff bled through some, my dad said, but at least the front-end loader could pick them up without everything…well, falling apart, I guess you'd say." She took a handkerchief from her sleeve and patted her brow. "My, my. I hadn't thought of all that in such a long time. It makes me sad even now, after all these years."

"I'm sorry to dredge all this up," Landry said. "Just a few more questions. After they cremated the bodies, did they bury them? Is there a cemetery somewhere?"

"If there is, those bodies weren't buried in it. The men had endured more than they signed up for at that point. They made sure the fire was good and hot, they stayed with it until flames reached high into the sky, and then everyone went back to their homes. All they wanted was to put what happened that day behind them, forever. People say nobody ever went back after that."

"Do you think the town's haunted?"

"With all respect to your work, Mr. Landry, I don't believe in that sort of thing. I do think when tragic events happen on a large scale in one place, like a hurricane wiping out the entire population, it puts those thoughts in people's minds. Even I've wondered sometimes if there's evil at work there. Who would want to go back to Midnight Pass? My parents had different ideas, though. They called it the Devil's Workshop."

He thanked Emma for the information, but before he left, she said, "There's one more thing, Mr. Landry. One of the people who disappeared down there was a woman named Natalie Hatcher. It was four or five years ago, I guess. She came in here looking for some relatives who died in the hurricane, and we talked for a while. I warned her not to go because of all the stories people told about mysterious things happening. There's nothing there anymore, and I worried she'd find more than she bargained for. Maybe get hurt or killed poking around all that rubble, you know what I mean?"

Interesting, Landry thought as he drove south out of town. *That lady Emma likely was the last person to see Natalie Hatcher alive, and even though she claimed not to believe, she warned her not to go.*

All the way down, he wondered if he was going to the right place, what he should be looking for, and what he would find. He arrived at the barricade to find a black-and-white Chevy Tahoe parked there. The words *Monroe County Sheriff's Department* were emblazoned on both sides, and the vehicle was empty and locked.

They sent a deputy up from Key West to look for Jack, Landry thought as he pulled his Jeep around the barrier for the third time and carefully proceeded along the narrow, swampy roadway that dead-ended at the fence outside Midnight Pass. "Hello? Anybody here?" he yelled as he walked through the archway into the town. The only answer came from the wind whispering through the empty, blackened shells, its tremolos rising and falling like the chanting of a ghostly choir.

How is it that the weather always changes when I set foot in this place? Thirty minutes earlier the day had been bright and sunny, but within the confines of Midnight Pass, ominous rain clouds swelled overhead, and a chill hung in the air. He rounded a corner, then another until he came to the square where the cremation had taken place, and again he called out. This time someone answered—a faint, distant voice.

"Over here. Where are you?" They traded shouts until they met on a street Landry hadn't seen earlier, a residential block with collapsed carports draped over antique automobiles, and yards filled with Radio Flyer wagons, tricycles and barbecue grills. Each bore silent testimony to lives that once had been, but ended on one fateful afternoon.

A stocky man younger than Landry walked to the intersection where he stood. He wore blue jeans and a dark shirt with a badge. A holstered service revolver and a radio hung from his belt. "McCarty," he said, approaching Landry with an outstretched hand. "Deputy Tim McCarty. Nice to meet you, Mr. Drake."

"Uh, did you know I'd be coming here?"

"Yes, sir. Chief Hawkins up in Everglades City radioed me to keep an eye out for you."

Interesting, Landry thought. *I went to the museum, but I didn't stop by city hall this time. Word travels fast in a small town.*

"I saw your SUV; you're from Monroe County. Did you drive up from Key West?"

"Yes, sir, the day before yesterday. With the recent…uh, activity here, the sheriff thought someone should be stationed up here for a week or so. I'm based out of Chief Hawkins's office, but I'm spending most of the daylight hours here."

"What have you found so far?"

"Absolutely nothing. The sheriff says there has to be an explanation for the people disappearing. It's not supernatural or anything like that, and he told me to look all over town to find someplace a perp could be hiding out. Maybe he's one of those swamp people—crazies, you know, who hide out in the Everglades and assault unsuspecting tourists. Or a prison escapee. Something like that. I know that probably doesn't jive with what you think, since you're a ghost hunter and all that. But those of us in law enforcement have to deal with hard evidence—you know, real stuff. There's an answer to this, and I hope we find it before someone else gets hurt."

Landry smiled at the condescending description of hard evidence. He'd been there himself, and he knew the drill. But he also understood that hard evidence might not provide the answers. Sometimes you had to open your mind and consider things that defied explanation.

"Does the sheriff think those missing persons are dead?" he asked, and the deputy nodded. "I'm not supposed to discuss it with people in Everglades City. Don't want to get them scared or anything, but yeah, the boss says we're more likely to find bodies than the living. Otherwise, the missing people would have turned up by now. Makes total sense, don't you agree?"

"In my business, I have to think outside the box," Landry replied diplomatically. "I've been here twice and found nothing out of the ordinary. It's an eerie place where an enormous tragedy occurred, but so far nothing else. But now it's personal. The latest one to disappear…"

"That newscaster from Louisiana? Jack Blair?"

"Yes. He's a good friend. We used to work together, and I came as soon as I heard."

"Well, I hope you have more luck than I have so far. If you don't mind my asking, what's your plan?"

Landry admitted he didn't have one, but he couldn't sit in his office while his friend was missing. Knowing he had to do something, here he was. Interrupted by the vibration of his phone, he took a call from Cate.

"Are you in Midnight Pass?" she asked.

"Yes."

"Landry, listen to me. You have to be careful. Henri just found out something that concerns me. You remember that guy we saw there who worked for the Department of Transportation?"

"Sure. Buddy Elkins. What about him?"

"I was telling Henri all about our visit, and he asked if we had seen the man's truck. Was it at the barricade? Or on the narrow lane that required four-wheel drive? Or parked at the fence outside town? No, it wasn't. We never saw his truck at all. That piqued Henri's interest, and he made a call. Landry, there's no one named Buddy Elkins working for the Florida Department of Transportation."

He paused a moment, considering. "So what you're saying…"

"What I'm saying is, as harmless as he seemed and whatever he was up to, that man wasn't who he claimed to be."

"How about when he advised us not to mention the devil being at work here because we might regret it?"

"That was weird," Cate agreed, but Landry wasn't listening. He was focused now on the armed officer standing ten feet from him, waiting for him to finish the call. Was he really Deputy Tim McCarty, or another impersonator?

CHAPTER FOURTEEN

"Check something else for me, Cate," he said evenly into the phone as he kept his eyes fixed on the deputy and the weapon on his belt. "Call the Monroe County Sheriff's Department in Key West. Ask them if they have a deputy named McCarty, and if he's currently assigned to duty in Midnight Pass."

"Are you…are you with that person right now?" she asked. "Landry, what if…"

"Just do it. Put me on hold; I'll wait."

Alarmed, the young deputy fidgeted uncomfortably. "Uh, Mr. Drake, have I done something wrong?"

"Last time I was here, I met a man wearing a uniform who claimed to be with the Department of Transportation, but it turns out he wasn't. I don't know what that was about, so I'm just being cautious. Someone from my office is going to confirm your identity."

"Yes, sir. Of course. I get that. I guess I should have asked you for ID too, since I'm supposed to be guarding the town." He laughed nervously. "But then again, I knew you the minute I saw you because I've seen you on TV. Guess that's the difference between you and me." Another nervous twitter. "Oh gosh, I don't mean…I mean, I'm nothing like you. You're famous and stuff, and I'm…"

Cate came back on the line, and Landry nodded. "Things are fine, Deputy McCarty. I'm me, and you're you, and we're all good."

"Okay, that's a relief! I couldn't help overhearing your conversation. You said something about the devil being at work in this town. Is that what you think's going on in Midnight Pass, that it's the devil's workshop?"

Landry assured him that snippet of conversation wasn't about his own thoughts. Another person had said those words—an impersonator whom Landry and Cate had met in the town a few days ago. Given the deputy's assignment to investigate Midnight Pass, Landry told him everything about that encounter in case it turned out to be something useful. For the rest of his visit, he walked the desolate streets with McCarty, repeating the things he knew about the hurricane, and showing the officer the pyre where Landry believed the mass cremation occurred.

"When you came the other times, did you get the feeling someone was watching you?" the deputy asked as they walked the streets. "Since I came, I've gotten that sensation a few times. Kind of a creepy feeling, you know? Like there's somebody else here besides me. Once I thought I saw someone—an old guy with a ball cap, wearing bib overalls like a farmer would. He was standing off down the block, and then he was gone. It happened so quickly, I might not actually have seen him at all."

A few minutes later a bell rang out through the town, tolling the hour. "Eleven on the dot." McCarty glanced at his watch, then saw Landry running off down a side street. "What are you doing?" the deputy cried. He caught up a block away and huffed, "What's up? Where are you going?"

"That bell! How can there be a bell? There's not a

building left standing in the entire town."

"Look over there!" the deputy cried, pointing. "Look at that huge bell!"

Still framed inside the spire where it once towered over the Catholic church, the old bell now lay in a pile of debris where it had collapsed. Landry and the officer stared at it, knowing it hadn't pealed in over eighty years. Although physically impossible, there was no mistaking what they had heard, and that it had happened precisely on time.

Deputy McCarty looked to the paranormal expert for an explanation or at least a theory, but he got neither. "Given this dream I had, I half-expected to find the church still standing," Landry admitted, and McCarty pushed him to explain. When he heard about the old Iberia Parish sheriff office somehow situated here amid the rubble, the deputy said, "I wasn't going to bring it up for fear you'd think I was nuts, but something weird happened to me too."

On his first day in Midnight Pass, McCarty had been walking through town, panning his iPhone right and left to create a video. He sent it off to the sheriff in Key West without reviewing it, and towards the end of the day, his boss called.

"How come I didn't hear from you after you sent that video?" Sheriff Warner had asked. "Didn't you think we should talk about what you found?"

"Sir? I…I didn't find anything, Sheriff. The whole town blew away, and nobody ever came back. It's just like it was in 1935."

"Except for that one building, right? You shot video of it; how do you think that drugstore managed to survive the storm and look fresh and new when everything else got obliterated?"

Deputy McCarty wasn't sure what to say. He had no idea what his boss had seen, and he said so. "There's nothing left in Midnight Pass," he repeated, and his bewildered superior told him to watch the video and call him back. McCarty did just that, looking closely at twenty-two minutes of footage and seeing nothing but devastation. Now he wondered what to do. The sheriff expected a callback, but what was McCarty to say—that his boss was seeing things?

He chose his words carefully, telling Sheriff Warner about the eerie sensations he'd felt since he arrived in Midnight Pass. The camera on his phone might be faulty, he suggested, or some other glitch might have caused an aberration. But one thing was certain—there was no "fresh and new" drugstore in this desolate town.

The sheriff's response had surprised McCarty. "I want you to spend the next two days there like we planned," he had said, "but then come on back. I understand what you're saying about eerie sensations. I'm a hundred miles from there as the crow flies, but something's not right in that town. We've done our duty. Give it a couple more days and get out."

Sheriff Warner explained why he felt so uneasy about the place. The building caught on video couldn't be standing amid the rubble in Midnight Pass because it was a scene from another time and place. "After we talked, I took a screenshot of that building and printed it off," he continued. "It seemed familiar, and when I looked closely at the name painted on the front window, it gave me the willies. Baxter's Drug. Forty years ago my folks and I lived in Emporia, Kansas, and Mr. Baxter was our druggist." The sheriff had paused a moment, as if considering whether to reveal more to his deputy, then continued, "Somehow I saw that building because it was connected to my past, even though it isn't there."

"My boss is a tough, old-school guy," the young deputy said. "He's an ex-Miami cop, and he's hard as nails. He would never make up a story like that, but if he says he saw that building, I believe him. And then something even weirder happened. The video showing the building disappeared, according to the sheriff. Just vanished like it had never been there. Same thing happened to his screenshot and the print—both blank. Mr. Drake, how the hell is that possible?"

"How the hell indeed?" Landry mused. He'd had a similar experience, seeing the old Iberia Parish sheriff's office here, but Warner's revelation was one more unsolved mystery. What was up in Midnight Pass?

Wanting time alone to explore, Landry suggested they split up and meet back in an hour. He wanted to see what he might turn up by walking the entire length of the iron spike fence that formed the village's perimeter. Thunder rolled through the dark clouds overhead, and a light rain began to fall as he worked to keep to the fence line, sidestepping broken chairs, tables and personal items strewn about in the backyards of what had been people's homes. Depression swept over him as he saw sadness and ruin everywhere he looked.

He got a text, glanced at the screen, read what was displayed and grabbed for the fence to steady himself. The terse message from an unknown caller consisted of just two words, and he knew without question who sent them.

Find me.

CHAPTER FIFTEEN

His fingers flew over the keys. *Where are you?* He waited impatiently. *Are you OK? In Midnight Pass?*

Landry's frustration grew as the seconds ticked by. One minute, then another with no reply. What should he do? He'd answered Jack's message within seconds, so why hadn't he heard anything?

Where are you? he typed again, punching the send button hard as if that would ensure its delivery.

A thousand thoughts swirled about in his head as he struggled to decide what to do. There were parts of Midnight Pass he hadn't seen yet, but every block looked just like the last. Then again, maybe somewhere in town—on a side street or in an alley—he would find an answer. He ran back to the square and shouted for Deputy McCarty.

"I'm over by the church!"

Landry found the deputy sitting in the middle of the street, unpacking things from what looked like a large rectangular toolbox. "What are you doing?" he asked, and the deputy said he was assembling a drone the sheriff had sent with him.

A drone! Exactly what we need! Landry dropped to the ground next to McCarty and offered to help. He explained about the text and the silence that followed. This drone might be the answer; it could surveil the town much more quickly than they could walk it, reveal anything out of the ordinary, and maybe point them to Jack Blair.

Soon Deputy McCarty had the controls in his hand and was maneuvering the craft slowly above the streets of Midnight Pass. Landry held the officer's iPad, watching the scene being transmitted from thirty feet overhead. McCarty flew the drone in a grid pattern, traversing each street north to south from one end of town to the other. Every block was the same as the rest, and after half an hour, he brought the machine down and asked if Landry wanted to keep going. He said he'd like to finish the grid while they were here and had the equipment, so McCarty replaced the drone's drained battery with a fresh one and sent it back into the air.

They began with the northernmost street, starting at the beach on the west end of town and moving slowly along until they reached a marshy area that lay just beyond the fence boundary on the east. One monotonous pass, a turn and a pass back continued until the craft reached the square with the funeral pyre. It had continued to the end, made another turn and started along the next street when Landry shouted, "Stop! Something's going on!"

McCarty set the drone to hover in midair and glanced at a white screen. "What happened?"

"The screen's blank. Everything's been fine, but a minute ago it stopped transmitting. Think that replacement battery's okay?"

"Yeah. We use this thing a lot. It's not the battery. Let's keep flying and see if it fixes itself." Twenty seconds later the video feed resumed, and Landry asked him to mark the coordinates where the blip occurred. After finishing the street search with no further issues and no new information, the deputy brought the drone back.

"Let's find the place where the video feed stopped," Landry said, and when the unit was safely back in its case, they set off down the street. The location was several blocks away, and just as McCarty said, "It should be around this next corner," Landry's phone dinged. Unknown number.

Help me!

"Come on!" Landry yelled. "We have to find him!"

They sped around the corner and kept going until the officer said, "Stop! This is where we lost the video."

It was a carbon copy of the others—no modern building nestled between ruined ones, no shop from the past beckoning them to come inside—but they still walked one side of the street, then the other from one end of the block to the next.

"Nothing," Landry muttered. "What are we missing?"

McCarty grabbed his sleeve and pointed. "Look way off down the street. Do you see the old man dressed in overalls? That's the guy I told you I saw earlier." Through the tendrils of fog that swept through the streets, Landry could just make out a figure. He took a few steps in that direction, but the man, if he'd been there at all, had disappeared.

Pausing, Landry cocked his head. "Listen! Do you hear someone talking?" The muffled sound of a male voice came from some buildings behind them. Landry ran to one, then the next, and cried, "It's coming from that building! I think it's Jack! Jack, I can hear you. We're coming to rescue you!" He raced toward the dark entrance, dodging bricks from its facade that now lay in a jumbled heap.

"Don't go in there! It's not safe," McCarty yelled. "The slightest movement might cause the second floor to collapse."

"I have to do it. I can hear him. He's in there..."

Landry paused and strained to hear the familiar voice. There was no question it was Jack, but something was wrong. Coming from somewhere deep in the old structure, the muffled words became more distinct as he stepped inside the building and listened.

...and overnight guests at the Myrtles Plantation still claim to see the spirit of Chloe roaming the halls...

What the hell? Landry looked around the dark, shadowy room. He couldn't see much, but he knew the words were Jack's because he had heard those words before, in another time and place, at the end of a television broadcast about a house in St. Francisville Parish. Jack had narrated the show, and it had aired on Channel Nine. Landry remembered the words because Jack had asked him to critique this milestone, Jack's debut on-air piece as an investigative reporter.

This is Jack Blair for WCCY-TV, the Voice of the Crescent City.

Landry didn't know what to do next. Were the texts really from Jack? How could dialogue from Jack's show be coming from inside a dilapidated building? Why did the drone footage go blank in this particular place? Where was Jack, and was he really in trouble?

"Maybe it's not him texting," the deputy offered. "What if someone else has his phone and they saw your name in his contact list. You're famous, and maybe they're playing some kind of cruel joke by texting and pretending to be your friend."

"It's not a joke. Something's very wrong here. He's somewhere in this town, and he's trying desperately to reach out to me. I have to find him before..." He walked to the entryway of the old building, pushed aside some boards, and stepped over the threshold. The deputy listened a moment as Landry clomped and crashed around, then went in after him. He had no desire to go inside, but he had to help. He pulled his service revolver and stepped through.

CHAPTER SIXTEEN

The old building creaked and groaned as if it were alive. As he moved deeper inside, Landry worried that each step might bring down a rickety wall or part of the ceiling that hung in shreds above his head. Sidestepping between long tables, he realized this had been a department store: signs advertised Dickey and Lee work shirts and pants, and rotting piles of cloth that had been outerwear and skivvies lay where they had been displayed for sale.

Once Deputy McCarty was in, he saw Landry twenty feet in front of him, standing in front of another doorway, using his phone flashlight to peer inside. Afraid to speak for fear the noise would trigger an avalanche, the deputy holstered his pistol and whispered, "I'm coming with you."

"No. Stay back. It's not safe."

"It's as safe for me as it is for you." He pushed ahead as Landry stepped out of sight and cursed when he bumped his shin against a table leg, sending open boxes of cuff links crashing to the floor. "Landry," he called as he reached the second doorway and pulled out his own light.

There was no reply.

"Landry!" he cried louder as he walked into a room filled with appliances, record players and radios displayed below cards tacked to the walls bearing descriptions and prices. McCarty saw Zenith, Kelvinator, Maytag and GE appliances, and as his eyes adjusted to the half-darkness, he noticed the dim glow of a light ten feet away. "Landry, are you there?"

"Shh! No noise!" Landry stood before an RCA Victor radio the size of a microwave, turning dials as he shone the light on its face. McCarty watched a moment, asked what he was doing, and Landry explained that there was something different about this radio. Every other appliance in the room was covered in a thick layer of dust. Some lay on the floor where they'd fallen when their display tables collapsed. But one—only this one—was as clean as if someone had taken a dust cloth to it moments earlier. Landry turned the radio around and saw a maze of glass tubes of varying sizes, wires and little metal boxes, all of which appeared shiny and pristine.

"I just happened to notice this one. It uses electricity, of course, so it won't work, but I'm wondering why it's in good shape compared to everything else in here."

"Would it work if you plugged it in?" the deputy asked, and Landry thought probably so, as long as the wire hadn't been gnawed by rodents. He picked it up and ran his fingers down the cord. It was perfect, of course. Just as perfect as the radio to which it was attached.

"Those words—that TV show—they couldn't have come from it, right?"

"Of course not. TV signals from the twenty-first century couldn't come through the speakers of a 1935 radio that has no power."

"So what do you make of it?"

"I don't know. In my world, some things aren't

easily explained away. I have a gut feeling Jack's broadcast did come from the radio. Let's see if we can get this thing out of here without bringing down the building around us."

The machine was more bulky than heavy, and they carefully maneuvered it across the showroom floor and out into the front room. As they carried it toward the front door, Landry became aware of a movement on his right in the darkness.

"Hold up," he whispered. "Put this thing down. Something's over there." He raised his light and directed it to a piece of furniture—a sales counter—along one wall. He saw something move again in the shadows and took a step in that direction.

Suddenly a row of chandeliers dangling precariously from the ceiling flickered to life, illuminating the store with an eerie grayish glow. Taken by surprise, they both yelled when the radio crackled to life.

This is Jack Blair for WCCY-TV, the Voice of the Crescent City.

This is Jack Blair for WCCY-TV, the Voice of the Crescent City.

This is Jack Blair for WCCY-TV, the Voice of the Crescent City.

They became aware of a man standing behind the counter across the room. He wore a red-and-white striped vest that made him look like a singer in a barbershop quartet. Had he been there all along? Neither knew, but at this moment—and perhaps *only* at this moment—he was as real as they.

"Hey there, gents!" he called out jovially. "I see you've picked out an RCA. One of our most popular models, she is. I'm sure you're going to enjoy your new radio!"

The words came much louder this time.

This is Jack Blair for WCCY-TV, the Voice of the Crescent City.

Landry delivered a strong kick into the back of the machine, crushing the innards and sending a wisp of smoke and glass tubes and wires flying everywhere. “Where’s Jack?” he yelled as he sprinted across the room to the counter. But no one was there; the man had vanished.

The radio crackled to life. Through mangled speakers ripped from the chassis and lying crushed on the floor came the same eerie words.

This is Jack Blair for WCCY-TV, the Voice of the Crescent City.

This is Jack...

The madness ended when Landry dropped a piece of cinder block on the radio, annihilating the machine he had thought might somehow lead them to Jack.

Moments later, Landry and the visibly shaken sheriff’s deputy stood in the street. McCarty said, “How...what the hell happened in there? How did that radio keep going, and how can it be possible...”

“None of it’s possible. What’s happening is outside the realm of reality. Don’t even try to explain it.”

“I don’t understand. Are you saying I just witnessed a paranormal event?”

“Call it whatever you want—a paranormal event, the gateway to another dimension, a dream sequence played out in real life, a time warp—what it is doesn’t matter. What matters is that Jack’s missing, and I feel I’m being taunted, like it’s a game.”

“Because you’re a ghost hunter?”

“I don’t know. I just feel it.”

The deputy asked if what they’d experienced inside the building was real. “Real?” Landry thought a moment. “We don’t use that word much in my business. You and I saw and heard the same things—the clean, new radio that worked without power and broadcast TV audio, the chandeliers that illuminated by themselves, the man who spoke to us—so those things were real in a sense, I suppose. They seemed real enough at the time, although do you agree with me that none of that was logically possible?"

"Sure. So you're saying it wasn't real."

"We experienced it, so in one way it was real, whatever that means. I try not to overanalyze things that defy explanation in the first place, because it's a waste of time. People in my field search for meanings behind the phenomena, and we try to figure out what it is we're up against. This one's on me, of course. You have no role in this; the battle is between me and…whatever. You need to get as far away from here as possible. While you can."

"What do you mean by that? If somebody's kidnapped your friend or if you're the target, I have to stay and help. That's my job."

Landry shot him a rueful smile. "If it were only that simple. I haven't scratched the surface of this mystery, but this town is nothing like it seems. Behind the facades of hurricane-ravaged buildings, behind the cremation pyre, I believe something is waiting for me. It knows I'm here, it teases me with glimpses into the supernatural, and now it's got my friend. One thing's clear—this is no ordinary kidnapping by some criminal looking for a ransom. I've dealt with the paranormal for years. No lawman and no conventional weapon are going to stop what's happening in Midnight Pass. This place is a cursed madhouse—a whirlwind of unexplainable things that affect each person in a different way—and for it to end, I have to face the entity that's causing everything to happen. And I must do it alone."

CHAPTER SEVENTEEN

Landry and Tim McCarty left as the sun was setting. The deputy caught a ride in the Jeep back to the barricade where he'd left his SUV, and when Landry said he was coming back tomorrow, McCarty promised to return too. First, this was his assigned post; second, he was excited but a little apprehensive about helping the famous paranormal investigator work on a case. Landry again cautioned him that nothing here was what it appeared, and he would be best off returning to Key West. But McCarty was hooked and wanted to help. They agreed to meet at the barrier at eight.

After a quick dinner and a long, hot shower, Landry called Cate and filled her in on the unusual things that had transpired in Midnight Pass. She thought he should call for more policemen, but once he walked through the folly of that idea, she gave up. The law enforcement people who were nearby had no jurisdiction. The ones who did were hours away, except for one deputy, whom Landry promised to keep by his side despite knowing the young man would be helpless to intervene if the supernatural manifested itself. Landry too, for that matter. Although knowledgeable about the paranormal, he had no powers against the dark forces other than his wits, intuition and cunning.

At seven the next morning Landry had just ordered breakfast when Cate called to say she had an errand for him.

"An errand? I'm heading back to Midnight Pass in half an hour. What's this about?"

"It involves making a little detour. You'll get to Midnight Pass; you're just going to be a little late. I need you to make a run to the airport in Fort Myers."

"I can't, Cate. I have things to do today. I'm meeting the deputy. There's no time…"

"If you leave now, you can be there by 8:30. The plane arrives at nine, and you can be back to Midnight Pass by 10:30."

"Whose plane? You're not coming down here. Things are getting dangerous…"

"My point exactly," she said. "I'm not coming; I'm sending Phil. He can help you keep an eye on things; plus Henri and I think it's time to shoot some footage of the town. We agree with you there are unexplained things going on, and we think it's time to think about turning your experiences into a show."

After getting past her interrupting his work and deciding on her own to send reinforcements, Landry gave in, thinking having Phil Vandegriff along wouldn't be such a bad idea. A seasoned cameraman who had worked with Landry at the TV station before joining them at the new Paranormal Network, Phil had witnessed some of Landry's most harrowing adventures, capturing video of supernatural phenomena that became episodes in the *Bayou Hauntings* and *Mysterious America* series. And along with their being colleagues, Phil was one of Landry and Cate's best friends.

Landry headed north on US 41; although he wouldn't make his eight o'clock rendezvous with Deputy

McCarty at the barricade, he couldn't let him know since they hadn't exchanged numbers. He could have relayed a message through the sheriff's office in Key West, but he decided the fewer people who knew about his business in Midnight Pass, the better. He'd be two or three hours late, that's all.

He met Phil curbside, loaded his equipment, and on the return trip, Landry had plenty of time to fill in his friend on recent events and his plans for the day. At 10:45, they passed the deputy's SUV at the barricade and shortly arrived at the fence outside Midnight Pass, where a rumble of thunder in the dark clouds announced Landry's arrival.

"Damn, this is one spooky place," Phil commented as they unloaded the Jeep. "Killed all of them in one afternoon, eh? If that doesn't invite paranormal activity, I can't imagine what would." Landry helped Phil tote his gear to the square, shouting McCarty's name but seeing no sign of the man. He pointed out the storefront, described the radio episode yesterday, and peeked inside to confirm it still lay on the floor where he'd crushed it with a block. Things, like people, had a way of disappearing in Midnight Pass, but the demolished RCA radio still lay where it had fallen.

While Phil unpacked his equipment and prepared for their first video shoot, Landry walked through the town, shouting for Deputy McCarty and Jack. The words echoed between the hollow buildings, but there was no response. Half an hour later Phil texted that he was finishing up a drone flight and was about ready to kick things off.

Phil had flown a drone over the town for ten minutes, and he scanned the footage before starting the shoot with Landry. As Deputy McCarty's drone had shown, every block had been dealt with equally; there were no pockets where a building or two had been saved. Regardless of where the residents might have sheltered, the results would have been the same—complete and utter destruction.

The usual low-hanging clouds and sharp wind created an atmosphere of forbidding gloom, which Landry considered a perfect backdrop for today's shoot. He stood in front of the cremation pyre, introducing viewers to the ghost town and describing the catastrophe. As Phil followed with the camera, he pointed out the collapsed buildings and explained how workers had stacked lumber and timber into a pile, tossed the wrapped bodies on it, and set it afire. And then he talked about the reason he was in Midnight Pass today—like several others over recent years, another person was missing. This time it was his friend Jack Blair.

When the first segment ended, Phil did the usual, reviewing the footage to ensure he was satisfied with it. Any retakes would happen immediately, when they were still in place and the information was fresh. As he worked, Landry again wandered off and called for the deputy and Jack. He heard Phil's shout and found him staring into the camera screen.

"Some kind of glitch happened while I was filming you. I rewound it, so take a look." Landry watched himself talking about Midnight Pass when without warning, a bright flash of light obliterated the feed. A split second later, normal video resumed.

"What happened?"

"I don't know. That's a first, but something else is going on too. So much weird stuff happens when I'm with you that I occasionally ignore things, but this is personal. There's footage on here that's only about me, and I don't get it. Take a look here—it begins after that brilliant flash of light." He paused the video on a certain frame, zoomed in on Landry until his face became blurry, and said, "Check out those buildings over your left shoulder."

Phil made an adjustment that brought the background into sharper focus. There, sandwiched between razed structures, stood one that defied explanation. Glass panes filled its windows, native stone faced the two-story building, and a tall, narrow sign ran from above the door to the eaves. Its letters, fashioned in red neon, spelled out the word PENDERGRAFT'S. Below the sign, a man held the door open as a family walked in.

Like the sheriff's office in Landry's dream and the drugstore described by Deputy McCarty's boss, Phil had filmed a building that didn't belong in Midnight Pass—an intact, well-kept structure from another place and time. It wasn't really there, of course; every building on that side of the street was as dead as the next.

"Why do you say it's personal?"

"I know that place. I've gone into that building hundreds of times, right through the front door under that tall sign where Mr. Pendergraft stood behind a counter inside and welcomed everyone to his cafeteria. It was in Monroe, Louisiana. We went every Sunday after church; you'd get your tray and go through the line. I have wonderful memories of it; Mom and Dad would let me pick out whatever I wanted, which usually meant getting two pieces of the best coconut meringue pie in the world.

"What's going on here, Landry? Pendergraft's was torn down forty years ago. It isn't here, of course. It never was, but just after that flash of light, it appeared in my video exactly as I remember it."

"I can't explain what's going on," Landry said, "but as I mentioned, you're not the first; the sheriff saw a drugstore from his childhood back in Kansas. Mine came in a recurring dream about the sheriff's office in New Iberia where I once worked. Both were here in Midnight Pass, sandwiched between collapsed buildings like yours was. At least we have confirmed proof now. You got it on video." Then he thought of something he'd seen. "Hey, wind it back to where that family was going into the restaurant. Remember there was a man holding the door open for them? I want to look at that frame again."

Phil froze the frame and enlarged it. There was nothing remarkable about the figure. He'd doffed his Astros ball cap to the lady who was going into the restaurant, and he wore a blue flannel shirt with bib overalls and thigh-high work boots. He was just another resident of Midnight Pass—a farmer, from the looks of him, commonplace and nondescript and just going about his own business.

When Landry finished, Phil made some adjustments but then said, "Damn, that's weird. All that just disappeared. The flash of light and Pendergraft's Cafeteria aren't there. The old man and the family either. It's just you describing the town straight through. No interruptions, no unexplainable building."

"What? You didn't get it?"

"I got everything—you saw it. One second it was there; the next it wasn't. I've never had that happen before."

"I guess nothing should surprise me anymore," Landry said. "I should be terrified or puzzled or something, but it seems all I'm doing is searching for Jack and waiting for the next inexplicable thing to happen."

CHAPTER EIGHTEEN

As Landry showed him the town, Phil pointed up and said, "Look, a drone," and watched Landry run into the middle of the street, wave his arms wildly and shout, "We're here! We're here!" As the craft banked to the west, they followed until they came to the boundary fence and the gate that led onto the beach, where they found Deputy McCarty coming over the large sand dune that separated Midnight Pass from the ocean and toting the case with the drone.

"I missed you this morning," he said after Landry introduced Phil. "Weren't we supposed to meet at eight? I was worried something might have happened to you." Landry explained that he had no contact information—something they immediately remedied—and he had made a run to the airport to pick up his cameraman.

"Frankly, I was a little worried myself," he admitted. "Your vehicle's up by the barricade, and when we didn't see you in town, I went all over looking for you. I must have shouted your name a hundred times."

"Sorry. I was down on the beach. The wind's really

picked up, and I couldn't hear you. I hadn't reconnoitered that part of the area before, so I took the drone and checked it out in case there were any clues about your missing friend. Nothing to report, I'm afraid. When I flew it back over the town, I saw you waving."

"Was everything quiet when you got here this morning? No strange sightings or phenomena?"

"Dead as a doornail. Weather was great too until about an hour ago when all these clouds popped up. Hey, wasn't that about the time you guys arrived?" Landry nodded, pointing out that the weather always turned when he came to Midnight Pass. Why, he couldn't say, but there was no denying it. Just one more mystery to add to the list.

"I halfway expected to see some storefront from my past like that drugstore I caught on my phone the other day," McCarty said, which led Landry to explain about the mysterious video footage Phil had captured and then lost.

"Are we dealing with a form of past life regression?" Phil asked. They had encountered that curious phenomenon in the French Quarter building that had become their headquarters. The event, memorialized in a Bayou Hauntings episode called "Die Again," involved spirits who inhabited the ancient building and a girl who learned through hypnosis she had lived as another person long ago.

Landry disagreed. "I think they're flashbacks, perhaps triggered by some repressed memory. I can't understand why it happened to three unrelated people, but if we can figure out the secrets in this place, maybe we'll learn what part the memories play."

McCarty advised that tomorrow would be his last day because the boss had ordered him back to Key West, but for Landry the work here was just beginning. He asked Phil's opinion about bringing Henri down, along with a set of complex equipment the Paranormal Network used to monitor and record unusual events.

"I don't have a vote about which projects you tackle," Phil replied, "but all the strange stuff going on makes it clear there's paranormal activity here. Even the weather changes when you come to town. Throw in Jack's disappearance and it's a slam dunk. I say go for it."

Twenty-four hours later, just as the investigation into the strange events at Midnight Pass was set to shift into high gear, things began going awry.

CHAPTER NINETEEN

Taken individually, that morning's occurrences were the hiccups travelers encounter every day. But that many in such a short time seemed to indicate a pattern that Henri Duchamp thought unusual.

On the morning he was to fly to Fort Myers, Cate took Henri to the New Orleans airport. They loaded six crates of equipment on two baggage carts and paid overweight fees, which Cate claimed were highway robbery. He boarded a full flight, and once the forward door closed, the plane backed away from the jet bridge and taxied to a line in which the pilot announced they were number sixteen for takeoff. As the minutes ticked by and the plane inched forward, a summer squall moved in, which was typical for a humid morning on the Gulf Coast. Soon lightning streaked through the sky as the low-hanging clouds unleashed a torrent of rain.

"Sorry, folks," the captain said through the overhead speakers. "Lightning and takeoffs don't mix, so every plane in line is returning to the terminal until the storm passes." For almost an hour, the passengers sipped on free cocktails as the heavy rain continued. Once it became a drizzle and the skies began to clear, passengers were asked to buckle up and prepare to taxi out. The plane rolled to the active taxiway and joined a much larger line, but when it reached the end where it should U-turn onto the runway for takeoff, the plane instead moved aside, allowing others in line to take its place.

"When it rains, it pours, I guess," the captain announced, knowing his passengers wouldn't be happy about what he had to tell them. "We've got an indicator light flashing up here in the cockpit. We're going to have to return to the terminal so maintenance can take a look. Shouldn't be too long if it's something minor."

Henri watched several passengers angrily punch their cellphones as they worked on alternate arrangements, but he knew Fort Myers was a once-a-day destination for this airline. You might connect through Tampa or Miami or Orlando, but any way you looked at it, if they didn't go soon, he'd be on this same flight tomorrow.

And things played out in exactly that way. Maintenance showed up, spent almost an hour doing whatever they did, and the pilot apologetically told everyone the plane was being taken out of service. Since New Orleans wasn't a hub, there wasn't an available spare in a hangar somewhere, so the flight was cancelled. There were no others that day, so Henri called Cate, who came back, helped him load the crates into her SUV, and took him back to the office.

The news disappointed Landry, who couldn't afford to be away from the studio much longer. Now he faced a wasted day without Henri along to investigate. Leaving Phil shooting background footage, he went off to explore the west boundary of Midnight Pass—the sandy dunes and shoreline outside the iron fence. He topped the high dune and saw a beach littered with plastic bottles, seaweed and debris that had swept in from the Gulf. He stepped aside when he caught a whiff of a dead fish lying near the waterline.

A sudden gust threatened to snatch away his cap; he grabbed it just in time and turned to walk back into town when he saw someone coming along the beach in his direction. He waved, and the person—a boy who looked to be around twelve—waved back.

"Hi, mister," he said when they were close enough to be heard over the wind. "Whatcha doin' out here?"

"I was wondering the same thing about you. Where'd you come from?"

The boy said his family lived in a fishing shack about a mile away, and he often walked on the beach, looking for things of value that might have washed ashore. "Nobody ever comes here, so I find good stuff sometimes. How about you? I think you're the first person I've ever seen on this beach."

"I'm just looking around. I heard the story about Midnight Pass…"

"Which one? There are lots of stories."

"About the hurricane that wiped out the whole town."

"Yeah, that. Everybody died in one afternoon. Crazy to think about, huh? They bulldozed everybody into a big pile and set 'em on fire. That must've been wild. Wish I'd have been there to see that!"

His enthusiasm over the gory event surprised Landry, but then he was a kid, and kids sometimes exhibited a notable lack of discretion and tact. "I figure it was a pretty sad afternoon," he said. "Those workers probably never forgot what they saw that day."

"Whatever. Anyway, nice to meet ya. Don't let the devil get hold of you in Midnight Pass!" He started off down the beach.

Landry called after him, "What? What's that supposed to mean? Hey, kid!" But the boy just waved and kept walking.

Guess he's heard tales about the devil riding the hurricane into town that day, he thought as he walked back through the arched gate. After another hour vainly shouting for Jack and peering through the entrances to old buildings, he gave up for the day. Emotionally drained from the constant searching with no results, he told Phil to pack up. They were going back to Everglades City.

Along the way he kept an eye out for turnoffs that might lead to a fishing shack where a family lived. Since it was lunchtime, he told Phil about a place he'd heard about called the Havanna Inn on Chokoloskee Island. They crossed a bridge and found what he expected—an authentic island dive bar—a thatched-roof open-air joint with Buffett on the speakers, grouper on the menu, and Red Stripe in the fridge.

While they waited for their meals, he called Chief Hawkins, told him about meeting the boy, and learned there were no fishing shacks—or residences of any other kind—within miles of Midnight Pass. Everything around that spit of land was swamp, and the child could not have lived anywhere close by.

So how did he get to the beach, why did he lie, and who was he?

After lunch, he and Phil returned to the Ivey House. With a rare afternoon free, they sat by the pool, Landry trying to read as his mind replayed one unexplainable event after another. Nothing in Midnight Pass made sense, and nothing was as it should be. Was there an explanation? He was beginning to wonder.

Soon he'd begin to find answers from a most unexpected source.

He must have dozed, because around three he became aware of nervous giggles and whispers nearby. He raised his head from the chaise longue and looked at Phil next to him. "Two old biddies found a celebrity!" he said. "They've been eyeing you ever since they came outside."

He sat up as one of them gave a timid wave, stifling a groan as one shuffled over. "It *is* you! I told Maddie it was! What on earth are you doing in Everglades City, Mr. Drake? Oh, and may I have your autograph? I have paper in my purse."

He sidestepped her first question. "Sure you can. What are you ladies doing down here in the swamps?"

"We're birders, actually. There are some species in the Everglades that aren't found anywhere else in America. We took an airboat ride yesterday, not to see the birds, of course. Those loud engines scare away everything but the alligators. We saw one of those, by the way. He looked more lethargic than vicious!"

Landry yawned, then apologized.

"Oh, I'm talking too much, aren't I? Maddie says I do that, but I'm just so excited to meet one of my favorite TV personalities! Speaking of that, are you on another ghost-hunting mission?"

He feinted again. "This is an interesting area, and we're just looking around to see what we might run into."

"I'm surprised at that! I wouldn't think you'd have time to just go puttering around places. Don't people send you suggestions?"

"Yes, ma'am, and that's what we're doing here. We're investigating some old tales about the area." He looked at his watch. "I have to make a call in a few minutes. Wanna go get that paper so I can sign it?"

"That was clever," Phil smirked as she tottered away. "Who you gonna call, Ghostbusters?"

Landry chuckled. "I had to think of something, but now we have to go inside."

"Not me, buddy. She's not one bit interested in me. It's all about you, her 'favorite TV personality'!"

CHAPTER TWENTY

In New Orleans the next morning, Cate and Henri repeated the airport run, and from his window seat, Henri watched luggage handlers load the underbelly of the aircraft. His carryon bag was stowed overhead, and he counted his crates as they were hoisted onto a conveyer. One, two, three, four…

He looked at the cart that held the remaining luggage, but the other two crates weren't there. As the flight attendant made a final trip down the aisle, checking for buckled seat belts, he asked about them. She took his claim tags, went to the front galley, and didn't return until the plane backed out and rumbled off to the taxiway. She handed him the checks and said, "Mr. Duchamp, I'm sorry, but there's nothing we could do. With the captain ready to go and a full flight, we couldn't delay our departure. I'm sure your luggage will be fine. If it's not already on board, it'll be sent down on the next flight and delivered to you. Go to the service desk in the baggage claim area, and they'll sort it out."

Henri thanked the attendant, knowing that without

all of his equipment, the trip to Midnight Pass might be a bust. There was nothing she or anyone else could do about it, and with only one daily flight, any missing crates wouldn't arrive until the next morning, and that was if everything went well.

He settled back, opened a book, and tried to let it go. Maybe he'd missed seeing them load the first two. That was his best-case outcome, but the reality turned out as he'd expected. Two of his six boxes of equipment still sat in New Orleans, and rather than having them sent to Fort Myers, he opted to retrieve them when he returned home. He wasn't certain what the missing ones held; he just hoped the other four had sufficient gear to gather the information Landry wanted.

Landry was waiting in the airport's baggage claim area. Since the Wrangler had limited cargo space, he had rented a small U-Haul trailer to transport the boxes. At the barricade near Midnight Pass, they opened each crate, and Henri took stock of what was missing. Some of the tracking gear that monitored unusual sounds and movements hadn't made it, but other cameras and sensing devices were there. Henri said that data collection would be hampered somewhat, but overall, things were far better than they could have been. He and Landry unhooked the trailer, stowed the empty boxes inside, packed the rear seat of the Jeep full of equipment, and drove off down the path.

Earlier, Landry had given Henri a list of the places where odd things had occurred: the block where Sheriff Warner saw a drugstore from his past in a video, the store where a radio played Jack Blair's signoff on WCCY-TV, the church bell that chimed the hour while lying in a heap of rubble, and the street where Phil Vandegriff's camera captured a cafeteria from his childhood, only to have it vanish. Those places would be the first where Henri would set up his audio-video sensing devices.

Leaving him, Landry guided Phil through the

streets, pointing out places and things he wanted to get on video. They stopped for an occasional voiceover and rejoined Henri when he texted that his gear was ready. "I placed equipment in the four places you reported unexplained phenomena, and I'll let things run for an hour. Fortunately I had the motion- and sound-activated equipment and some of the electromagnetic measurement gear. Fingers crossed that we get good results."

When Henri saw the mound of charred lumber that Landry had dubbed the cremation pyre, he thought it would be an excellent place to set up his equipment. So many bodies and so much tragedy concentrated in one place might make the sensors go wild.

As they walked through residential streets, Henri was fascinated to find an entire town frozen in time. Landry had seen some of it earlier—nineteen-thirties-era automobiles sitting in collapsed one-car garages attached to Depression-era two-bedroom-one-bath bungalows. If one ventured inside the ruined houses, Henri wondered, would they find food on the table or dishes in the sink from Labor Day lunch in 1935? The destruction was so complete that such exploring would be dangerous, although Landry thought it would be interesting to see what they'd find. After all, he'd been told nobody ever came back to reclaim anything. These homes would indeed have captured a moment in time more than eighty years ago.

Everyone helped Henri relocate his gear to the square. He positioned lights, cameras, and various sensors around the cremation pyre, turned everything on, and checked the gauges. Phil filmed Landry and Henri as they walked the town and pointed out interesting things among the rubble—the car dealership with the latest models in its showroom windows; the huge bank vault door that might or might not be locked; the church steeple lying in pieces, its bell impossibly tolling the hour when least expected.

"We should have a go at that vault door," Phil said.

"It's the most intriguing thing I've seen because it's protecting the only room in town that could have withstood a hurricane."

Landry agreed. "Cate and I talked about the vault on our last trip. Those houses might have food still on the table, but everything's buried under collapsed roofs. I think the vault is likely intact, and it'd be fascinating to see what's inside, but we can't risk it. Those walls are just too unstable."

"Where there's a will, sometimes there's a way," Phil said with a wink. "Let's don't give up on it just yet. Leave it to me."

Camera running as they walked back to meet up with Henri, they rounded a corner and got a surprise. Next to the only three-story relic left standing were Maddie and Priscilla, the senior-citizen birders from yesterday. The ladies appeared surprised but also overjoyed to have learned Landry's secret.

"We caught you in Midnight Pass! I should have figured that out when I first saw you!" Priscilla said, rushing over to give Landry a hug. "This is such a spooky place. Have you found any ghosts yet?"

He grinned. "No, not yet. What are you doing here? Can you find birds in collapsed buildings?"

"Oh, yes, you can! We're looking for the grasshopper sparrow, a bird that's rarely sighted anywhere, but its natural habitat is here in south Florida. I think we've found a nest way up there in those ruins across the street!" She looked through her binoculars and said, "Quiet, everyone. We may see them any minute."

"We'll leave you all to it," he whispered, and Maddie suggested they meet up for a glass of wine later. He waffled, saying he wasn't sure when they'd be back. From now on, he'd need to stay alert to avoid running into his new best friends.

———

After Deputy McCarty had been recalled to Key West, Landry became increasingly frustrated at the lack of concern on the part of law enforcement. Each disappearance in Midnight Pass mattered, especially Jack's, which was top priority for Landry. But sitting a hundred miles away, the sheriff in Key West seemed to have no interest in solving the crimes. In a conversation that had begun cordially, Landry bluntly informed Sheriff Warner that Midnight Pass was in his county whether he liked it or not. "I've gotten more cooperation from the Collier County sheriff in Naples than from your office," he added.

"Listen, I sent a deputy up there for four days. He found nothing. I don't have the resources to spare him any longer."

"I understand you saw something unusual in a phone video. Something from your past that made you decide to recall Deputy McCarty."

That struck a nerve. The sheriff sputtered, "He had no business…listen up, Mr. Drake. Your interests and mine are way, way different. You believe in ghosts and all that crap, and you're out for the sensationalism. Your friend Jack Blair is a newsman just like you. My deputy found nothing going on in Midnight Pass, and it makes me wonder if you all cooked up this disappearance so you could create an interesting TV show."

Struggling to control his temper, Landry realized the deputy hadn't said anything about hearing Jack's voice coming through a 1935 RCA radio or seeing a man dressed in a fancy vest behind the counter who was there one minute and gone the next. Obviously Deputy McCarty had taken the path of discretion instead of irritating his boss, whom Landry now considered to be a hotheaded jerk.

He said, "With all due respect, Sheriff, Jack's only the most recent of several people who went missing. You've never found even one of them. You've hardly investigated, from what I can see."

Sarcasm dripped from every word. "Thanks for your assessment of my department's investigative work. Even though you're not from south Florida, you have swamps back in Louisiana. When you mess around in the Everglades and don't keep your wits about you, shit can happen. Gators drag people into the water, and that's the end of the story. Happens more often than you'd think. Listen, you stay in Midnight Pass for as long as you want, looking for spooks and creepy crawlers and whatever else it is you ghost hunters do. If you find any evidence—anything at all to indicate a crime has been committed—then you call me back. Otherwise, I have better things to do."

"What's more important than looking for a missing person?" Landry snorted, but the lawman was already gone.

When he repeated the conversation, Phil suggested it was better this way. "Do you want some nosy deputy keeping tabs and reporting back on everything you do? Whether he meant to or not, the sheriff gave you carte blanche to do whatever you want, so let's tear this place apart until we figure out what's going on."

PART THREE

THE VAULT

CHAPTER TWENTY-ONE

By late afternoon they'd collected considerable data from the two sites, which Henri downloaded to his laptop. Landry said they should leave soon, since the narrow lane back to the barricade would be dangerous to cross in the dark.

"My equipment has around four hours of battery life remaining," Henri said. "Why don't we leave it running and see what we get? Maybe we can learn something about Jack's whereabouts. I'll set up security cameras to keep an eye on the equipment." Henri checked each device a final time, and they walked back to the Jeep.

They kept to their rooms until six, used the side exit to avoid the ladies, and walked two blocks to a restaurant the owner of the inn recommended. A connoisseur of fine food and wine, Henri huffed at the mostly fried entrees and house red and white wines on the laminated menu. Landry quipped, "It's the best place to eat in town, and wine's a bargain at six bucks a glass, fourteen a bottle. At least they don't pour it from a box."

"My heavens, what a ghastly thought." Henri

summoned the server and asked if it was allowed to bring one's own bottle of wine. The manager gave the okay, and he left the restaurant, returning a few minutes later with a bottle.

"2011 Châteauneuf-du-Pape," he said, handing the bottle and an opener to the waiter. "One of the best vintages of the twentieth century. Handle it carefully. It's quite...well, let's just say it's a very nice wine."

"I've never heard of this one," the young server said as he inspected the label and eased out the cork. "Is it good?" Henri assured him it was "good" and took back the bottle, saying he'd do the pouring himself.

Nothing about the scene surprised Landry; Henri appreciated the finer things in life, and on a trip to the boondocks, Landry would have been more surprised if he hadn't packed his own libation. Phil, however, who knew Henri mostly from work and was unaware of his sometimes pompous behavior, was caught off guard. "You brought your own booze? Does it cost more than six bucks a glass? Did you bring enough for everybody to have a taste?"

Henri huffed, "You couldn't buy a sip for six dollars, and yes, I'll share." Henri felt comfortable with the offer, since Landry and Phil already had glasses of the house white sitting before them. He presumed they'd stay with theirs instead of taking some of the expensive French red.

"I'm a cheap date, so I'll stick with the cheap stuff," Phil said. "By the way, have you tried the Boone's Farm '23? It's exquisite, with a firm nose or broad shoulders or however you describe wine." Henri guffawed and said he'd have to take Phil's word for it.

Henri told them what he found when he reviewed the data he'd collected today. Although the devices picked up nothing specific, each had recorded significant aberrations that confirmed the existence of paranormal activity. It was literally in the air, seeping from every old building and manifesting the strongest from the cremation pyre. "The needles were jumping all over the place," he explained. "The whole town's literally bursting with energy. And we picked up audio from the cremation area—deep sighs and groans. I'll let you hear them later; there's no mistaking the immense sadness and pain. What an awful thing to happen to a town."

They talked at length about Jack. Despite the lack of progress since his disappearance, Landry refused to give up searching. The lack of clues in and around Midnight Pass was disconcerting, and they wondered if Jack had ever made it to town at all. He'd left his rental car at the barricade three miles away. Did someone accost him there or along the narrow roadway past the barrier? Could a gator have surprised him, or did he trip and fall into the swamp? Like the other missing persons, there was evidence he'd been in the area, so how and why did he vanish?

Landry told them about his recurring dream—the feeling that people had been burned alive that day, that Jack had been kidnapped so someone could get to Landry, and he described hearing Jack's pleas for help. "It was so real that I wonder…" He stopped, lost in thought.

They talked about people—Buddy Elkins, the man he and Cate had met in Midnight Pass who falsely claimed to be with the Department of Transportation. "He even had the uniform, and that made me wary about the sheriff's deputy from Key West, who turned out to be legit. Then there was a kid on the beach who claimed to live nearby, although nobody lives within miles of the place. What's the connection? Who's behind it, and what's the purpose?"

"Enigmas, for the present," Henri mused. "For the sake of discussion, let's assume we're dealing with a man and not something from the paranormal realm. What do you have that he wants? Publicity, maybe. His fifteen minutes of fame. If he's been kidnapping people since at least the late eighties, maybe he's irritated that the cases didn't end up making him famous. Maybe he's devised a way to go out in a blaze of glory and take you with him."

Landry listened, Henri might be correct, but something nagged at him—a piece of this puzzle they were missing. He wasn't gifted with extrasensory powers—a sixth sense—but he'd been investigating unexplained mysteries for years, and he had a hunch this wasn't the work of a kidnapper. Not everything in life had rational explanations. There were forces at work in the world that defied logic, and with its tragic, horrific past, Midnight Pass was an ideal breeding ground for the supernatural.

Back at the inn after dinner, they sat by the pool and laid out the morning's plan. First off, they'd check Henri's equipment and download any audio or video recordings from the night. Phil sat quietly, reflecting. He had a plan, but he'd wait until tomorrow to spring it on them, allowing them less time to talk him out of it.

Finished for the evening, they walked through the lobby to go to their rooms and were surprised to see the ladies sitting by a fireplace across the room. Priscilla said, "I hope you aren't angry with us. We stayed inside while you men were out there talking so as not to intrude. Landry, could you please take a moment to tell us a little about what things are happening in Midnight Pass? We're just fascinated. There's such a story there…my goodness, how haunted it must be!"

He had no easy out, so he agreed to talk with them for a few minutes before turning in. Relieved it was Landry the women were after, Henri and Phil waved goodnight and went to their rooms, wondering how long it would take for him to break free and come to bed.

CHAPTER TWENTY-TWO

The next morning Phil drove, stopping first at a hardware store, where he selected three hard hats, flashlights, light sticks, some tools, a grappling hook and a length of strong rope. He refused to answer their questions, promising to explain everything once they arrived. This time when they reached the archway that led through the spiked fence into town, Phil eased the Jeep past, drove carefully down the main street and stopped in front of the bank building. He killed the engine, and Landry said, "If you're thinking about pulling down the walls…"

"Exactly what I'm thinking," he replied as he checked the front winch bolted to the Jeep's frame. "I looked at the exterior yesterday. It's two bricks thick, and there's plaster on the inside. The ceiling has collapsed in several places, which takes load off the walls. It won't be hard to pull one down. Then we can remove some of the debris and get to the vault."

Henri shook his head, warned Phil to stick with his day job, and walked off to check the equipment he'd left running in the square.

Landry cautioned that it was too dangerous, but nothing deterred Phil, who unrolled several feet of cable from the winch on the Jeep, tossed the rope to Landry, and said, "Tie the grappling hook on here." He found a place to secure the hook inside a gaping first-floor window, tied the other end of the rope to the winch, and slowly retracted the cable until the line was taut.

"Put on your hard hat and move back. The entire wall may come down all at once." He put the Jeep in reverse, accelerated, and after straining for a moment, the grappling hook ripped away a large section of brick wall next to the empty window. Although every part of the wall shook precariously, the bricks above the gaping hole remained in place.

Phil prepared to replace the hook and repeat the process, but Landry refused to let him get close to the wall. It looked as if the slightest breeze would bring it down, but Phil asked for one more try and promised to be careful.

Landry shrugged and said, "Go for it. If you get yourself killed doing this crazy stunt, I'm going to be mad at you for the rest of the day."

Phil stepped cautiously through the debris around the wall, got as close as he dared, and swung the hook around and around before tossing it into the hole where the window had been. He missed once, then twice, but the third try was a success. When he tugged to check it was secure, a few bricks tumbled down, sending him scampering back to the Jeep. He reversed the Wrangler, pulled the rope taut, and accelerated. This time a much bigger chunk of wall came loose, bringing down a section twenty feet wide and opening a passageway through the exterior wall. It wasn't the safest way to get inside, but the risk of being struck by falling debris was greatly reduced. Still, a daunting pile of bricks, plaster and boards that lay strewn about inside and out remained to be negotiated before they could attempt to reach the vault.

They took a break and went to the square, finding Henri sitting on the ground, staring intently at his laptop screen. "Anything interesting?" Landry asked.

Henri's voice was low and tinged with sadness. "Interesting. Fascinating. Horrifying. The equipment went berserk after we left. Electromagnetic imagery, sounds, visions—the paranormal energy emanating from the cremation pyre was off the charts, more than I've ever seen. None of it's real, of course. I mean, it *was* real once, I think, but what my devices recorded is evidence the dead remain trapped in Midnight Pass. And take a look at this."

His cameras had recorded a huge bonfire created from an enormous stack of burning lumber, its flames, lifted by the wind, leaping high into the sky. The wood crackled and popped as the fire consumed the things on top of it—dozens upon dozens of shrouded things that resembled huge white cocoons.

"My God, this is incredible!" Landry gasped. "Do you think…are we seeing how it actually looked in 1935?"

"Undoubtedly. It certainly didn't happen last night; look over there; the wood is cold and charred, just as we saw it yesterday."

"I'm surprised you're so calm about this. This is unbelievable. It's video from eighty years ago."

"It's nothing compared to what comes next. Listen." He increased the volume; they could hear the crackling fire, the popping of burning lumber, but then came another sound—a muffled, mournful wail, hardly distinguishable over the noise of the pyre. Then a second, different in pitch and intensity, followed by another.

The usually stoic man looked up as a tear ran down his cheek. "Do you hear that? That's the sound of sheer horror. They wrapped people up in those shrouds, piled them on the wood and set the bonfire. Some of them were still alive, Landry. Just like you dreamed, they tossed people into the fire who weren't quite dead yet. Maybe they were unconscious, but what if the flames reached these pitiful human beings before the rescue workers left? They would have begun to hear the most frightful screams and wails, and they would have realized what a horrible mistake they made."

"They left, and nobody ever came back to reclaim bodies or property," Landry whispered. "The word must have gotten around, the workers would all have lived in neighboring towns, and they told their neighbors what they'd experienced. After that, nobody came back. No wonder they talked about the devil riding the hurricane in and doing his work here. It's true."

Phil asked him to reverse the video to a certain place; he'd caught a glimpse of something odd and wanted a second look. Henri restarted it, and it ran for a moment until Phil cried, "Stop there!" He pointed at the frozen frame and said, "Look at that. Explain that to me."

Around the funeral pyre stood the workers, who watched as a tractor stacked bodies upon the woodpile. Some distance back on one side stood two others. Henri zoomed in and enlarged the frame as much as he could.

The video was from 1935, but nearby, wearing the same hats and clothing as yesterday, stood two observers—Maddie and Priscilla, the bird ladies. They stood in silence and watched as the final bodies went on the pile and the fire was lit.

Henri said, "What on earth do you make of that? I wonder if my camera created a double exposure, somehow filming them yesterday and then superimposing it on the video of the fire."

"That's impossible," Phil said. "You don't have the equipment for it."

Landry stared at the screen. "Seems there's more to everyone we meet than we expect. If we see these ladies again, I'll have a few questions for them."

CHAPTER TWENTY-THREE

There was little communication as they walked over from the square back to the bank building. In his career as a paranormal investigator, Landry had seen awful things, some supernatural and some created by man, but this ranked among the saddest and most horrifying. To a skeptic, the video meant nothing. It could have been created in a studio, with fake flames and dubbed wails. But to Landry, Henri and Phil, it was as real as the day in 1935 when it happened.

Anxious to get to the vault door, Phil was first to break the melancholy. There was work to be done, and Phil told Landry and Henri to don their hard hats and follow him. "Watch for nails and stuff where you step," he cautioned as he navigated around bricks lying everywhere. Dodging more debris, they maneuvered across the room. A huge roof timber lay across the massive vault door; at the time it fell, they'd have needed the winch to move it, but it was so rotten now that a few jerks with the rope broke it apart. They moved other detritus that blocked the vault and created a space around it. The stainless-steel door held impressive dials and handles, all mostly free from rust and corrosion.

As Phil reached for a dial, Landry stopped him. “Don’t touch anything yet. Let’s see if it’s unlocked.”

“A bank vault? Why would they have left it unlocked?”

“What if people sought refuge from the storm in the one place that would still be standing after a category five hurricane? Waterproof, windproof—a perfect refuge. If they went inside, they would have pulled it closed but not locked it.”

Henri said, “No, but when the storm was over, they’d have locked it behind them.”

“Indulge me. Let’s try it before we start moving dials.” They grabbed handles and tugged, but the massive door didn’t budge. Phil suggested using the rope and winch, securing the hook around a handle and pulling with the Jeep, but Landry was afraid it would break the handle. He suggested finding someone online who knew about safe doors.

They saw the name MOSLER etched near the top of the door, and Henri searched the internet to find that Mosler Safe Company went bankrupt in 2001, and a company called Diebold acquired its assets. Landry placed a call that bounced around the company until they got a representative who listened to their story and offered to help. He asked Landry to shoot a picture of a metal plate affixed to the safe next to its largest handle. The man entered information off the plate into a computer and returned to the phone moments later.

“That was one of Mosler’s beauts,” the man said. “It’s also one of their biggest. Five thousand pounds, ten feet in diameter—a monster, but constructed so that one person could open and close it. Let’s see—the Security State Bank of Midnight Pass, Florida, bought the door in 1924. That’s the last record. Where’s the door today?”

“Still in Midnight Pass,” Landry replied. “It’s about

the only thing intact after a hurricane destroyed the town in 1935. We're trying to figure out if it's unlocked."

"Are you with the bank? There's a certain protocol—"

Landry interrupted. "I understand. No, nobody's lived in this town for eighty years. I'm an investigator..." This was a ploy Landry had used before. He was an investigator—a *paranormal* investigator—but that critical omission often led others to believe he was in law enforcement. "We're investigating several missing people in the area. I don't care what's in the safe. People have vanished, and I'm trying to find them."

"I see. Here's what I can do. If the safe's locked, then you can apply for permission to have one of our authorized representatives come open it. Since it's in a bank, you may have to get a court order. That can take time and be rather complicated, so let's check it out first. If someone left it unlocked, then there's no law against opening the door." He instructed them to jiggle a certain dial a little, to see if it was set on a number or would move freely. It was the former—a good sign, he said—and he instructed them to try the handles.

"This door can be closed from the inside," he advised. "You move the handles down, and it secures the door without locking it. They'd have remained safe and sound inside."

Landry asked how someone could survive inside with no air, and the man explained that there were two vent shafts high up on the safe door. Landry saw them—round and about the size of a tennis ball, with a wire net on the end. The collapsed ceiling beam had covered one; the other was open. "I don't see how you can get much air through those little holes," Landry said, and the man agreed, saying they were intended for short-term use.

While the rep remained on the line, Landry grasped two handles and gave a strong tug. The door moved a fraction, and the man said that was good news—the door was definitely unlocked. "Liberally apply oil or WD-40 to the hinges and rock the door back and forth. You'll get it open eventually." He wished them luck and disconnected.

"Where are we going to get WD-40?" Landry asked, but Phil was already halfway to the Jeep. "I saw those massive hinges yesterday," he said, returning with a can he'd bought at the hardware store. They squirted oil around the hinges and rocked the door. It went slowly, but the door moved a bit more with each try. At last it creaked open sufficiently to allow them to squeeze through. Landry went first, light stick in hand, but immediately broke out in a fit of coughing. He backed out and fell to his knees, frantically sucking in gulps of air.

"Can't breathe," he wheezed. "There's…there's no air in there."

"Come on, Henri. Let's crack that door wider," Phil said, squirting more oil on the hinges. He moved inside to push while Henri pulled on the handles. *One. Two. Three.* The door yielded, and soon it was sufficiently wide to allow air in and give them room to comfortably enter.

They found a spacious room lined on three walls with safety-deposit boxes. Small booths, each with its own table and chair, allowed customers a place for private access to their boxes. Two doors stood on the back wall—a wooden one and another in front of it that resembled a jail cell door with steel bars. Both were closed.

The room where they stood was a typical safety-deposit box area, the same found in hundreds of bank vaults, but one thing made this room something remarkably different.

That was the six bodies that were lying on the floor.

CHAPTER TWENTY-FOUR

Henri noted that the corpses were in a remarkable state of preservation due to the dry, airless conditions in the vault. Four women and two men, each with a light dusting of mold on their exposed skin. Four purses sat on a nearby table where the ladies had prudently placed them. Two suit coats hung neatly on the backs of chairs, ready for the men to wear when it was time to go back outside.

A girl in her twenties lay in the fetal position in a corner. Eyes bulging and mouth agape, her face captured her final moments straining for that last breath of air. A man of perhaps forty sprawled on the floor nearby. In an effort to breathe, he had loosened his tie before his end came.

Two middle-aged women in prim dresses—what Henri called suitable attire for bank employees back in the day—lay on the floor wrapped in each other's arms. Their countenances were calm, and Landry noticed a Bible next to one, still open to the twenty-third Psalm. These ladies had drawn their last breaths confident they were going to a better place.

The other man had received the worst of it. He had ripped away his collar, and bloodstains marked his starched white shirt. His bloody fingers still clutched his neck, where he had literally torn open his throat trying to get a last gasp of precious air.

The final body belonged to another female around thirty who wore a navy blue suit with a name tag. Nancy Stallings, Head Cashier. Like the two Christians, she had met her fate with calm resignation.

"It was smart of them to come in here," Phil whispered reverently. "The hurricane would have passed over in a few hours, and they should have had plenty of air to survive. Why didn't they leave when it was done?"

Landry replied, "Because that huge ceiling beam fell and blocked the door. We couldn't have moved the thing ourselves if it hadn't been so rotten. They couldn't get the door open. How horrible it must have been to realize the place they'd chosen for safety would instead be their tomb."

"But why was the bank open on Labor Day? And why did these particular employees get trapped? Why didn't they go home? Hurricanes give you plenty of advance notice."

Henri, who had been looking around the room, held up an old-fashioned stenographic pad he'd found lying on a table next to a radio. "I think we may find answers in this. Our Miss Stallings left a parting gift."

The head cashier had created a journal at the time they entered the vault. Henri read a few sentences from the first page.

Monday, September 3. 2:35 p.m.

Six of us are here in the vault. Two officers—Mr. Costain and Mr. Johnson—three tellers—Sandra Cox, Mimi Lanier and a girl named Sarah—I'm sorry, but I don't know her last name. And me. I'm Nancy Stallings, head cashier. I'm writing all this down just in case. I'm an optimist, but you never know what a hurricane can do. Maybe these thoughts will end up in my memoir when I get old.

We've known for days a hurricane was brewing, but every forecast put it west of us. When it struck Key West yesterday, the weather people on the radio said it would head west into the Gulf, but instead it veered to the northeast. Even though it was a holiday, Mr. Baxter asked us to work a short shift today because a lot of townspeople were preparing for the storm. Earlier, some had already withdrawn money and left town. I guess you could call them the smart ones. The remaining folks are the die-hards, I suppose. I helped out at the teller windows today, and each person in line wanted to tell the reason why they stayed. Many had ridden out storms before, and others were just too old and tired to leave. Some called it an adventure. I don't think I'd go that far. The interesting part is that the weather has been nice until an hour or so ago. I could hear the band playing in the square, they're still having a Labor Day celebration, and I guess they won't quit until it starts raining.

Mr. Fuller, the bank president, told us we could leave whenever we needed, but there were all those customers. Some wanted access to their safety-deposit boxes, and that took time away from the windows. Most were either withdrawing or depositing, and although most of the employees left when Mr. Baxter did, we six stayed on until the last customer had been helped. We hurriedly locked the tills in the safe, and Mr. Costain was just about to close the huge door when he paused, thank God.

By that time it was getting to be too late. The wind was blowing like crazy, and all of a sudden, huge waves crashed over the dunes, bringing water down Main Street and right into our building. We put sandbags outside the front door and gathered our belongings, but just as we were going to make a mad dash to the parking lot, a street sign came crashing through one of the huge windows that faced the street. A whirlwind of papers flew through the air. Maybe they were important, I recall thinking, but the only other thing I recall is that it was too late to care about papers. We had more to worry about now because we weren't going anywhere until the storm passed through.

The young teller, Sarah, cried about her dog being home alone as Mr. Costain ushered us all into the safe to ride out the storm. The vault could survive a direct hit, he told everyone, but when he said that, several people began weeping. We listened to the radio station in Naples, and the weatherman said the storm was a category five and heading straight up the coast. It was expected to make landfall south of Naples around two thirty.

We are south of Naples, and we came inside the vault and closed the door at fifteen past two. Mr. Costain assured us the door wasn't locked; he even showed us how to move the handle up and push it open. We listened to the radio and learned that Midnight Pass took a direct hit about ten minutes ago, but I guess Mr. Costain was right. This was a perfect place to ride out a hurricane. Here inside the vault it is as quiet as…a tomb. the lights went off a few minutes ago, and two battery-powered safety lights up in the corners came on.

The radio station in Naples just went off the air, which we know means the storm has hit there. Mr. Costain thinks it should be safe to take a peek outside and see how things look. He goes to the door, moves the handle and pushes. Nothing happens, and he tries again. Now he's calling Mr. Johnson to come help push, and we all pitch in. But the door won't open.

Why? That's the question on everyone's mind, and Mr. Costain says maybe the wind pushed the big table in the lobby in front of the door. He tells us to stay calm; there's an emergency telephone hidden inside the vault for just this kind of situation. Some of the others look hopeful, but I know it's not going to work. He opens a recessed drawer next to the safety-deposit boxes, takes out a telephone, and picks up the receiver. Nothing, because we just got hit by a hurricane. The realization that we are in serious trouble hasn't hit the others yet, but it will.

4:45 p.m.

It's been two hours. Some cry, some pray, some sit lost in thought, and I write. It keeps my mind off the inevitable. If people rescue us a day or two from now, my notes will be a reminder of how it felt to be locked in a vault. If no one comes...if no one thinks to look inside the vault, then it will be a memorial.

Mr. Baxter will come later on and get us out, Mr. Costain assures us. But that assumes Mr. Baxter, whose frame house sits two blocks from the water's edge, doesn't need rescuing himself.

6:20 p.m.

The air's beginning to get stale in here. Mr. Johnson is having some kind of panic attack; he's talking to himself and rocking back and forth in a corner. Sandra brought in a Bible; she and Mimi were reading passages aloud until Mr. Johnson shouted for them to stop. The devil's in here with us, he keeps saying, and he doesn't want you talking about the Bible. The girls just turned away from hIm, and now they're whispering verses to keep each other calm.

A few minutes ago the new girl, Sarah, asked what was behind that barred door in the back. Mr. Costain told her it was the inner sanctum—the place where the bank's cash and secure documents were stored. That's where we keep the tills too, but Sarah's not been here long enough to get to carry her own till inside. I think Sarah was hoping that door might be a way out. But it isn't.

7:45 p.m.

The first of the two battery-operated lights just flickered out, and the other one is on its last leg. I'll keep writing, even in the dark, for as long as I can put words to paper. The air is very thin now, and some people are struggling. Mimi, the oldest one of us at fifty-something, has asthma, and she is wheezing with every breath. I feel sorry for her and all of us, but at least she has faith. That should comfort her in what she will soon face, I fear.

Mr. Johnson keeps ranting about the devil being here. He shouts, "Hey, Satan! Come and get me!" Sandra yelled at him to shut up. "God's in charge here," she said, but it's hard for any of us to believe it, given our current circumstances.

8:08 p.m.

Mimi died so quietly her friend Sandra didn't know, even right beside her. When she realized it had happened, Sandra began praying, and young Sarah started screaming. Without a word of warning, Mr. Johnson leapt up from the corner, flew across the room, and slapped her hard. She fell back whimpering, and Mr. Costain pulled Johnson away, hitting him once in the face with his fist. With the air so thin, that exertion apparently was all it took, for Mr. Costain collapsed. Now he is dead too. There are four of us left, and one is a raving maniac we are all afraid of.

8:19 p.m.

The second light just flickered out. It is so incredibly dark I can't see the paper, but I keep writing, feeling my way along and turning the page when I think I have filled one. From here on, the times I use will simply be estimates, for I can't see my watch now. The air is so stale and thin that it's difficult to draw a breath. I call out names every two or three minutes. The last time I did so, Sarah didn't respond.

There are odd noises in the dark, but perhaps they're in my mind. I feel light-headed from lack of oxygen, and I'm not thinking clearly. There it is again—movement, someone shuffling around, whispers in the darkness, a voice I don't recognize—but I could be imagining all of it.

"Who's there?" I cry, and someone laughs. "Who laughed?" I ask, but no one responds. There's someone else in here with us. But that can't be true, can it? I think maybe it's just Mr. Johnson in some delusional state.

4 or 5 minutes later

Mr. Johnson begins to scream as if he were being attacked by some beast. Air! Air! He cries for the thing we all crave, but now there's a gurgling sound and a last feral cry. He is silent now. Sucking in gasps of air, Sandra asks if I'm a believer. "I like to think so," I reply, "but I don't know if Jesus believes in me." "He does," she assures me; then she says she has to sleep. And just like that, she's gone.

Here in the darkness it seems I am the last, but I know it won't be much

CHAPTER TWENTY-FIVE

The words in the journal painted a picture horrific beyond imagination, suffocating in the dark as others around you died. This vault had been a tomb for six people connected only by the place they worked. Had they not stayed behind to help the remaining customers, they would still have died, but perhaps the deaths of these six were the most painful. Maybe it would have been easier somehow to perish in the storm like everyone else in Midnight Pass.

Henri brought in several paranormal sensing devices and cameras, which he set up in various places around the vault. Like the cremation pyre, this room had a high concentration of energy, and he expected the results might surprise them.

"What do we do about the bodies?" Phil asked, and Landry said they'd stop by the police station in Everglades City. Chief Hawkins could figure out their disposition.

They had given the locked, barred door in back a cursory examination and found that it had a key lock. It also bore a metal tag with the same brand name as the vault and a number. Landry called his contact at Diebold, who said the cash vault was usually secured behind such a door, and from the journal they'd read, Landry knew that to be true. After Landry recited the number on the metal plate, the man said he could overnight a replacement key. "We're not allowed to pass these out to just anyone," he added. "But you said you're an investigator, right? What department are you with?"

Landry skillfully avoided a lie while also not answering the question. "Send it to Chief Ed Hawkins at the Everglades City Police Department," he said, reading off the address from his phone. That satisfied the safe rep, who said they'd have their key tomorrow. Now Landry had to convince the chief to cooperate.

They went back into the street and saw Maddie and Priscilla walking their way. "Oh, Mr. Landry, there you are! Have you had an interesting day?"

"I'm glad you've come," he said. "I want to show you something."

Henri took out his laptop and loaded the cremation video. He spent a moment finding the right frames, looked closely, frowned and tweaked some dials. "This is odd. Look at this." Henri started the video at the same place as before, but despite the three of them having seen the two ladies in the background watching the funeral pyre burn, they were no longer in the picture.

"How could that have happened?" Henri said, mostly to himself.

Landry replied, "This isn't the first time something's vanished from a recording. I'm not that surprised."

"Is everything all right?" Maddie asked. "Did we interrupt something?"

Landry approached them and snapped, "I don't think you've ever said where you're from. And where did you park your car when you came today?"

"Have we done something wrong? We didn't

mean…"

"Answer the questions!"

A look of alarm crossed Maddie's face. "Oh, my dear. We…uh, we're from Preston, Georgia. It's a tiny little place…"

"Where's your car?"

"It's…uh, we parked it a few miles back where the road ends. There's a big highway sign there blocking the way."

He turned to his friends. "There's only an hour until sundown. Henri, is everything set up for tonight?" It was, and Landry said he'd drive the women back to their car. Phil and Henri walked, since there wasn't room in the Jeep. As they approached the barrier and saw no car there, he asked them where they'd parked it.

"Just over there," Priscilla said, pointing to the right. Still seeing nothing, he drove around the sign and pulled over. As everyone got out, he looked around and said, "Where? I don't see your car. Where did you park it?"

The bird woman didn't reply. Neither did her friend Maddie, because Landry was alone.

He drove back down the path and picked up Henri and Phil. The unexplainable things were happening so frequently now that nothing surprised anyone. The only thing that was certain was that nothing could be taken for granted. Things that appeared normal were anything but.

Landry thought there might be security camera video of his talking with the women in the lobby last evening. Other guests might have seen them. Both were long shots, since these two birders were anything but what they claimed to be. He'd talk with the inn's manager when they returned.

They stopped first at the police station. Chief Hawkins was stunned to hear what they'd found in the bank vault and promised to take it from there. He'd call the Monroe County sheriff and arrange the disposition of the six corpses. This was unprecedented territory, six people had died eighty-seven years ago, but none was ever reported missing because the heirs assumed all the bodies had been cremated. The bodies had turned up, and an effort must be made to notify next of kin. That would be a chore easier said than done.

The chief was happy to turn over the safe key to Landry when it arrived, but Landry requested he be present when they opened the door. "According to the journal, that room contained the bank's cash and important papers. Most likely it still does, and I don't want to be responsible for the bank's property, even after all this time."

"I agree with the logic, although I doubt you'd have anyone challenge you, since the bank's been out of business for almost a century." Regardless, doing it by the book ensured that there would be no challenges later for Landry and his network. Hawkins said, "I'll be there if it's okay with Sheriff Warner. Otherwise, you'll have to wait until he sends somebody."

An hour later when they were at dinner, they received word that the chief would be their man. When the key was delivered tomorrow, he'd meet them at the barricade. He added that he was looking forward to working with Landry. Despite his earlier vow never to return to Midnight Pass, the new revelations were exciting, and he wondered what secrets might remain in the old town.

At the Ivey House, the night manager didn't recall two ladies from Georgia, nor were they registered guests. Landry said, "I sat on the couch over there the night before last and chatted with them. You were behind the desk. Do you remember?"

"I didn't pay you any attention because I was watching the ball game on TV," he admitted. "I did see you three gentlemen come through the lobby from the pool area and go to your rooms, but I don't remember your talking to anyone else. Let's check the cameras."

They hunched around a monitor in a cramped office and viewed footage. The three of them entered the lobby and talked for a moment before Landry turned his back and walked across the room. Henri and Phil went to the hallway that led to the bedrooms.

Landry sat on the couch, seemingly engaged in conversation, moving his head and lips and gesturing with his hands. In a few minutes he stood, appeared to speak again, gave a little wave, and walked to the hall. It surprised the manager—but not Landry and the guys—that for the entire time Landry had sat and conversed, he had been alone. During the entire time he was on camera, not another soul was around.

CHAPTER TWENTY-SIX

They drove back after breakfast the next morning, and the moment they arrived, Henri rushed into the vault to check his equipment. Everything stood exactly where he had placed it, the batteries had run down, but that would have no effect on the information captured beforehand. He took the devices out into the sunshine, connected backups, and began downloading the data, a job he estimated would take an hour.

While Henri was working, Chief Hawkins called to say FedEx had delivered the envelope containing the Mosler key, and he was heading in their direction. Landry met him at the barricade; as they headed to Midnight Pass, Hawkins said the Monroe County sheriff had authorized him to take charge of the situation. If necessary, he'd send up a deputy, but as usual, it could take several days. "I've told the coroner's office in Naples about the bodies," he said. "Again, it's a jurisdictional issue, but he's agreed to store the corpses until Monroe County can pick them up."

Landry handed him the journal they'd found in the vault, and as he read the bank employee's account of their final hours, he whispered, "So sad, so sad." He admitted to being apprehensive as they passed through the archway and walked down Main Street. At the corner they found Henri and Phil sitting in the street with a pile of electronic gear and cameras around them. "We need to talk," Henri said. "Looks like some interesting things happened last night in the vault." Landry said he'd show Chief Hawkins the vault first and be back shortly.

The bodies lay just as they'd been found yesterday. "This is unbelievable," Hawkins said. "No matter how long I live, I doubt I'll see anything as bizarre as this again." He took the journal from Landry, reading passages as he knelt beside each corpse. "I want to put names with faces. These people deserve respect. Everybody talks about the hundred and sixty-two who died that day, but these six died too, and they were forgotten."

Back in the street, they gathered around Henri's laptop while he consulted notes and fast-forwarded to the relevant parts of last night's recording session. He explained he wanted to begin at the end. "The biggest takeaway from five hours of data involves that room behind the barred door. Now and then the equipment fluctuated so wildly that I thought something had gone wrong with my sensors. They also recorded movement behind the door. Impossible, right?

"The paranormal indices would register one out of ten, then spike to a ten within seconds, remain there for a minute, sometimes two, and then fall back to one again. This happened over and over. The energy forces behind that door were sometimes greater than my machines could capture. That's never happened before."

The idea of movement behind the door intrigued them. As Henri had remarked, it was impossible. So what on earth could it be? The vault itself had been locked for decades, and this back room was doubly secure—a vault within a vault. Could there be another way in?

"The chief brought the key," Landry said. "Why don't we open that door and find out what's behind it."

They entered the vault, and Phil filmed as Landry did the honors by inserting the small brass key into the lock. It slid in easily but wouldn't turn. He wiggled it back and forth and exerted as much pressure as he dared, but the key remained stationary.

A quick call to the Diebold representative confirmed that the serial number on the brass plate matched the key the man had overnighted, meaning the key wasn't the issue. Given that this back area would typically hold the bank's cash—as much as a million dollars at any given time—most bankers had the locks changed after the barred doors were installed. Most likely, the man advised, the prudent officers of the Security State Bank of Midnight Pass had done just that. "That means you're going to need a locksmith," he added, "and not just any locksmith. These doors have built-in security features. It'll take a Mosler specialist to open that door."

"Any idea where I'd find one?" Landry asked, and after a brief search, the representative said, "The closest one's in Tampa. Do you want his contact info?"

That disappointing news got even more discouraging when Landry called the locksmith. *A cash vault door in a bank vault, eh? Are you with the bank? No? What's the purpose of getting inside? A missing persons investigation in Midnight Pass, a town that was abandoned in the 1930s? What authority do you have? Yes, I understand the police chief of Everglades City is there, but does he have jurisdiction? No? Who does? Monroe County? I'm going to need approval from someone there. I can make the trip; it's about three hours one way to Everglades City. I'll charge you a flat day rate of a thousand dollars.*

"Cate's going to flip when she finds out you're about to spend a thousand dollars of the network's money,"

Henri said with a smile.

"Would if that were the only obstacle," Landry replied. "We've got to get permission from the sheriff in Monroe County. Think he'll give it to you, Chief?"

"He's been cooperative enough so far, but I have to admit we've had conflicts in the past. Stuff that happens in the Everglades is in his county, but he expects me to take care of it since I'm a few miles away and he's a hundred. I get it, but he can be a pain in the ass sometimes, to be honest. All I can do is ask."

When Ed Hawkins called yet again, Sheriff Warner was tempted to tell the guy where to get off, but someday he'd need another favor, so he listened. He knew all about the bank vault and the six corpses. He'd given the chief permission to handle things, but what he wanted now was different—authority to open the locked door that secured the room where the bank kept cash and important papers.

"Tell me something, Hawkins. Why are you wasting so much time on this? I realize not much goes on in that hick town you live in, but can't you find a shoplifter to catch, or a guy who ran your one red light in town?"

"Very funny, Sheriff. The truth is—"

"The truth is, you're all enamored by that ghost hunter Landry Drake. He claims his friend is missing, but he can't provide any proof. He tried to reel me in, but I don't have time for it. I guess he found somebody who does. There's one born every minute, they say."

Chief Hawkins took a moment to calm down. "As I was about to say, the truth is that for far too long the world has ignored all those people who died in Midnight Pass. When I saw those six bodies, I saw them as human beings, not as six more to add to the death toll. I believe Landry's friend Jack Blair is missing, because there have been others, as you well know, and I'm going to help find him if I can."

"What exactly do you want from me?"

"A letter authorizing a locksmith to open the door in the back of the vault and granting me authority over the situation."

"If you find anything interesting, you stand down and call me immediately, understand?"

"So you'll come up if we find something interesting?"

"I didn't say that. You find something, you call me, period. I'll send you a fax."

Landry took the officer back to his vehicle, and he returned to Everglades City to await the sheriff's fax, which he forwarded to the locksmith. An hour later, the chief called to advise him the man would leave Tampa shortly and come to the police station. Hawkins would bring him to Midnight Pass, and they should be on-site by midafternoon.

At three Landry went to the barrier to meet Hawkins and the locksmith. On the drive to Midnight Pass, the chief had told him there were bodies in the vault. "So we're dealing with a crime scene?" the man asked, and Hawkins explained how they'd come to be locked inside for eighty-seven years.

He hauled a large toolbox into the vault and eyed the metal plate on the barred door. "Mosler was a good company," he said. "It's a shame they went bust." He took out an enormous ring with hundreds of keys on it and began flipping through. Landry asked how long it would take, and he said it could be ten minutes, it could be an hour, depending on how long it took to find out which type of key he needed. He inserted one, then the next and then another.

Landry said, "I thought you guys pulled out the locking mechanism and reset it."

"On ordinary locks, I can. But these bank vault locks are burglar-proof. It shouldn't take too much longer to find the type." A few minutes later, on maybe the fortieth key blank, he inserted it and turned it right and left.

"Bingo," he muttered.

"Is it open?" Phil asked.

"Not yet. All I've done is learned exactly which tool I have to use."

He took out a stethoscope and a long metal pick with a notch on the end. He inserted the pick into the lock and moved it about as he held the end of the stethoscope against it. In a few minutes he removed the pick and scope and inserted the key he'd used earlier. He turned it to one side and pulled on the gate.

But nothing happened.

"That's odd," he said to himself. "Everything's right. The tumblers clicked into place. It's unlocked. So why won't it open?"

An hour later he packed up, admitting defeat against a Mosler lock for the first time in his career. "Something's screwy about this one," he added. "Even though it's unlocked, it won't release. I don't know how that could happen, because these locks don't work like that."

"So how do we get inside?" Landry asked.

"Bulldoze down the walls around it, I guess. I'd bet money you're not going in through that door."

They paid the man and sent him on his way. For the next hour they shifted rubble from around the block walls of the room, but they found no other entrance. Admitting defeat for now, they returned to Everglades City, leaving Henri's equipment set up to record and monitor for another night.

CHAPTER TWENTY-SEVEN

Landry's morning ritual rarely varied. When he awoke, he looked at his cellphone, and as he did this morning, he felt a lump rise in his throat. After Henri went to his room last night, he and Phil had stayed up until almost midnight, drinking wine and strategizing about Midnight Pass. Afterwards it appeared he'd slept very well, because he'd missed three text messages between two and four a.m. from an unknown caller.

Help me!

Help me!

Help me!

Jack! He's alive, and we have to find him! He threw on a T-shirt and shorts, ran into the hall, and banged on Phil's door until he opened it, dripping wet and wrapped in a towel. Landry showed him the messages and said he wanted to go back as soon as possible.

"Hang on a minute," Phil replied. "None of those cries for help came from Jack's number. I get why you'd think it's him, but you don't know that. Let's stick to the plan; I'll meet you and Henri at 8:30; we'll finalize things over breakfast and head to Midnight Pass."

It's him, Landry thought. *I'm certain it's him, and these cries for help mean he's alive and he's in trouble.*

"I want to tear that town apart building by building," he declared as they sat on the patio at the Island Café, and Henri said although it was a noble gesture, it was physically impossible to accomplish without heavy equipment. There was also the matter of permission; poking around in ruins, even pulling down a wall was one thing, but wholesale demolition would be something else entirely. Henri steered Landry into a rational discussion of what the three of them actually might accomplish.

Phil reiterated his earlier concern. "No question somebody's trying to get Landry's attention, and maybe it's Jack, but how can we be sure? You guys are here as paranormal investigators, and Midnight Pass is infested with the paranormal. That's no surprise, given the town's horrific past, but we know what to do when we're faced with the supernatural, because we have plenty of experience. No reflection on you, Landry, but we don't go off half-cocked, we watch our steps, and we make decisions as a team."

"No reflection on me?" he replied in mock surprise. "When have I ever gone off half-cocked or failed to include you all?"

"No response required." Henri laughed. "But let's get down to business. Those texts appear to be luring you back to Midnight Pass. But why now? We were clearly going back today anyway; my equipment's all set up in the vault. If it's Jack and he's trapped in the town, how did he get a phone, and why didn't he call you? If it's not him, then who is it, what do they want, and what happened to Jack? Those are the questions that face us." Shortly they headed south, each wondering if today would bring answers.

Once again, Landry drove the Jeep all the way to

the old bank building. He and Phil left Henri to check his devices, and walked to the cremation pyre, which Landry considered the catalyst for paranormal activity in the town. While Phil set up the recording equipment, Landry sat on the ground near the mass of burnt lumber, his fingers on his temples as he struggled to focus every part of his mind on Jack Blair.

Where are you? Are those messages coming from you? Are you in trouble? Tell me, Jack. Tell me how I can help you.

The ding of an incoming text broke his reverie. He looked at his phone. Another unknown caller had sent the words *3030 Knight Road, Memphis.*

He showed the message to Phil, who was as mystified as Landry. This time he hit "reply" and sent three question marks.

Find me.

Find you in Memphis?

There was no reply.

"What happens next?" Landry asked, and Phil suggested they talk to Henri. They found him in the street, puttering around the electronic gear he'd hooked up to recharge.

"Strange things happened last night," he said when they approached. "Two sensors didn't work because their battery cables were unhooked, and one video camera was turned from the cash vault door a hundred and eighty degrees to where we come in through the big vault. Those things didn't happen accidentally."

"Have you looked at the video? Maybe the culprit's on camera."

"No, that's next. I wanted to get the machines charging first. Did you see anything going on in the town?"

Landry showed him the text messages. "What do you make of these?"

"How about putting the address into Google Earth?"

When they did, they saw a modest frame house with a carport that needed a lot of TLC. Two junker cars sat in the backyard. Other houses down the block were no different; the area had seen better days.

Landry shrugged. "So we know there's a house in Memphis at that address. What does that have to do with us?"

"I have another thirty minutes of download," Henri replied. "The text is an address, and it must be relevant. Why don't you two take a stroll through the residential part of town and see if you learn anything?" Landry considered walking around a waste of time, but as weird as things had become in this town, anything might happen, so off they went.

Once they left the business district, the blocks were all the same. Where neighborhoods had been, six piles of rubble mixed with personal effects stood on either side of the street. Here and there a mailbox or a gate remained, a silent reminder of how gale-force winds sometimes spared the smallest things while wreaking havoc elsewhere.

After several turns exploring places they hadn't been, Landry stopped. "Listen. Do you hear that music? Let's go find it!" Landry took off, pausing at a corner to listen before turning down one block, then another. The music grew louder, and Phil grabbed his arm. "Do you recognize that sound?"

"It sounds like the calliope that plays on the steamboat *Natchez* in New Orleans."

"Yeah, but it's something else too. My first thought was of an ice-cream vendor."

They rounded the last corner and stopped dead. "What the hell is this?" Phil muttered.

"Don't ask me how this is possible, but I have a feeling we're on Knight Road in Memphis, Tennessee."

Phil looked to his right and left to remind himself this was still Midnight Pass, but before them lay a single block that appeared to have been transplanted. He'd guessed correctly; the music really did come from an ice-cream truck parked in the middle of the block. This street was ordinary, with small, neat houses, yards well maintained, and a car sat in almost every driveway. They weren't new—most were from the 1970s or 1980s—but they weren't clunkers either. There were people—a mailman walking down the sidewalk, a girl playing with a dog, a lady unloading groceries from her Oldsmobile 88.

Landry had guessed well too; a street sign noted this was the three thousand block of Knight Road. "Let's find 3030," he said, starting down the block as Phil hoisted his camera to his shoulder and began recording.

They found the house and saw two boys with baseball gloves playing catch in the front yard. Landry waved and so did they. "Hi, guys," he said. "Can I ask you something?" They walked over to the fence.

He went for it, hoping he wouldn't scare them off. "We're not from here, and I'm a little confused. Can you help me out? We're in Memphis, right?"

One of them looked at his friend and laughed aloud. "Yessir, you sure are."

"Work with me here. Tell me what today is. Day, month, year. There's a dollar in it for you if you answer right."

"Okay. It's June the twenty-third, two thousand and four."

A woman opened the front door and stepped onto the porch. "Jack! Artie! Is everything okay out here?"

"Yes, Mom. We're just helping these guys." She stayed on the porch, making sure all was well. Landry knew it was time to go.

He turned to the boy who'd done all the talking and said, "You're Jack Blair, aren't you?"

CHAPTER TWENTY-EIGHT

At the mention of Jack's name, the entire scene vanished, leaving them standing in the middle of a block of destroyed residences and wondering about the significance of what they just saw.

"How could you tell the boy was Jack?" Phil asked.

"The setting, for one thing. We've talked about his life many times. He was an Army brat until his parents divorced when he was nine, and he and his mother moved to Memphis. She barely made a living, he said, and they lived in a small but well-kept house—the one we saw. Also, the kid looked like Jack. I could see it in his eyes, his face. For some reason, we caught a glimpse of Jack as a boy. It must be related somehow to his disappearance, but I can't figure out what it means. Can you?"

He was fiddling with the camera. "Beats me, but I hope to hell I got all that. The camera was recording the entire time, but you know how many times we've struck out." He rewound, looked for a moment, fast-forwarded and repeated the process several times. "And it happened again. Ten minutes of blank white space. It looks like we were in a blizzard." Landry wasn't surprised; over the years Phil had recorded hours of paranormal footage, much of which became part of the episodes they aired, but as often as not, the functioning equipment captured nothing. It was a part of the paranormal process they'd come to accept.

They told Henri, who agreed it was unfortunate the recording had failed, and added, "I had somewhat better luck last night with my recording devices, because things were busy in the Security State Bank. We've read the head cashier's account of that afternoon, but it appears I captured the event as it unfolded. Audio, video, the whole thing. It's a heart-wrenching, graphic account of what damage a storm can do."

As they gathered around the laptop to watch, Landry remarked that it resembled scenes from an old-time movie. As before, the camera sat in the middle of the bank lobby, aimed at the vault, and the row of teller windows was visible on the left. Customers—men wearing fedoras, women in long dresses, even though a storm was imminent—stood in line as the female tellers handled their banking business. "People dressed up for the hurricane," Phil commented, but Henri said that was how it was in 1935. That was what they wore, even at home after dinner. You took off your tie or your dress when you went to bed.

He fast-forwarded to a scene where a woman took charge. She ordered a teller to lock the front door, and they carried their tills to her desk. "I'll confirm your totals, and we'll be out of here in fifteen minutes," she assured them.

"It's getting worse out there," a young woman cried. "I'm scared, Miss Stallings. Are we going to be all right?"

"Let me finish!" she snapped, and shortly she told the girls to put their tills in the vault. When they finished, a man—Mr. Costain, according to the journal they'd read—began pushing the large door shut. The rest happened just as the head cashier had written about it. A wall of water struck the building and breached the double front doors. The staff rushed to put down sandbags, but when a sign crashed through a window—all of this caught on Henri's video—everyone fled to the safety of the vault. The huge door closed from inside, and the employees, who thought themselves safe, were doomed a few minutes later when a common wall came crashing down, bringing the roof beams with it. One enormous timber fell against the back wall, blocking the safe door and trapping six people inside. There they would remain for eighty-seven years.

"My God," Landry whispered. "It was one thing to read about it…"

Henri shook his head while Phil muttered, "Tragic. It's just tragic."

It was difficult to accomplish anything else after what they'd seen. At last Landry called it quits, saying, "I can't spend any more time here today. Let's go back and get all this uploaded. If we end up with a show, this is going to be some of the most important footage we have."

Henri said he'd backed up the video to his laptop, it looked good, and everything should be good to go.

They drove back to Chokoloskee Island for lunch at the Havanna Inn. It had been a mentally exhausting day, one filled with questions about Jack Blair's whereabouts and his involvement with the paranormal visions of times and places from decades earlier. Later, while Henri opted for a nap, Landry and Phil drank a few too many beers lounging by the pool. That evening, hangovers already in the making, they ordered a pizza, ate it in the B&B's common area, and went to bed.

CHAPTER TWENTY-NINE

Come back. Come back to Midnight Pass and help me! Landry, come now!

He awoke with a shout, his flailing arms sending a nightstand lamp crashing to the floor. Drenched in sweat, it took a moment to orient himself. *I'm in the B&B in Everglades City, and so are Henri and Phil.* He looked at his watch. 2:09 a.m. Then he concentrated on remembering what had jolted him out of the dream.

He had been inside the house on Knight Road. Jack had been there too—not as a child but an adult. They had been standing in a tiny bedroom at the back of the house, the room that had been Jack Blair's.

I lived in this house for nine years, just my mother and me. After high school, I took architectural classes in college, but after three semesters I flunked out because I was more interested in drugs and alcohol. She kicked me out, I moved to New Orleans, and eventually I met you, Landry. You saved my life once; now you have to save it again. Midnight Pass is filled with surprises—things beyond your wildest imagination. I know why I'm here, and

I know you shouldn't ever come back here again. Not ever. But you must. I have to get you back here.

Come back now. Come back to Midnight Pass and help me! Landry, come now!

His mind reeling, he brewed a cup of coffee in the machine on the bathroom countertop. Jack was reaching out to him, but everything was a jumbled maze of contradictions. *He wants me to save his life again, he knows why he's in Midnight Pass, and he claims I should never go back, ever. But he has to get me to come there, and he needs my help.*

So what the hell's going on?

His initial inclination was to get dressed and drive to Midnight Pass, but as he considered the words Jack had used, he reminded himself this had been a dream, not a phone call. There had been dreams in the past that foretold danger, and his impulsive actions had gotten him in dire straits more than once. The only thing certain was that Jack had disappeared in or near the abandoned town.

Awake and alert after the coffee, Landry argued with himself. What would it hurt to go check things out? He could roust the others, but for what? Nothing, most likely. A fifteen-minute ride south, a quick look around, nothing but dead silence everywhere, and a fifteen-minute ride back. If he left now, he'd be back in bed by 3:30.

What would Cate say if she knew what he was considering?

Don't go there. Don't even think about that. She isn't here, and if she were, she'd say do what I think best.

No, that isn't what she'd say. She'd give me all the good reasons why I should wait until the sun was up and I had Phil and Henri with me. She'd say don't go alone at night to a place I already know is brimming with paranormal activity. It's too dangerous.

Good old Cate, he thought as he pulled on his jeans. *Always watching out for me. I'll be back before you know it.*

He grabbed the Jeep keys on the way out the door and drove south through the sleeping town. He passed the barricade and drove along the narrow pathway between the marshes, maneuvering carefully in the darkness. One misstep here and he'd end up in the swamp. He parked near the bank building, grabbed his phone and a light stick, and got out, wondering where to begin. He stood in the street, taking note of his surroundings as he slowly made a three-hundred-sixty-degree turn. Midnight Pass was quiet. No church bells, no cries for help, nothing at all except a dead town. A literally dead town.

Something caught his eye, a glimmer of light from inside the bank, and he crept over for a look. He peered in through the gaping hole Phil had made and saw the vault door standing ajar. Through the crack, a faint glow emanated from inside.

Landry shrugged off a shudder and a prickling sensation that ran down his spine. The corpses were gone, the Collier County medical examiner had taken them to Naples yesterday, but that gave him little comfort. From the time they'd discovered the vault, they had worried that someone might hear about the safety-deposit boxes and come to loot them. For that reason, they ensured the huge door was closed every night. Although they didn't dare lock it, at least a trespasser would find the massive door shut. It might be enough to deter others, but now it seemed they could have been wrong.

He watched the door for several minutes; as the light flickered, he wondered if someone was inside. The prudent thing to do now was to leave. Someone inside would have heard him by now, and they could be waiting. But there was the thing about Jack, the reason he was here in the first place. He had to keep going.

Trying to keep quiet while moving through the debris, Landry crossed the room to the vault door. From here the light seemed brighter, but the door wasn't open wide enough for him to look inside. He palmed his phone and stuck his arm through the opening, snapped a photo, and brought it back.

The room appeared exactly as it had when he last saw it, except for one thing—a candle in an old-fashioned brass holder, its flame dancing in the darkness, that stood on a table in the middle of the room. Although he couldn't see everywhere, it appeared no one was in the vault.

Then where did the candle come from? Go back, Landry. Go back to the B&B, get the others, call Chief Hawkins, and come to Midnight Pass with enough reinforcements to make this a fair fight...if a fight is what's brewing. Don't tackle this alone.

There's nobody inside. Sixty seconds to check it out. That's all I need. Sixty seconds.

He pulled on the massive door until he could step inside. He looked in every corner and under the tables, but no other living soul was in the vault. He looked closely at the candle; from the appearance of wax that ran down the holder, he figured it might have been burning an hour, maybe less. Someone left a signal for his arrival. This was all meant for him.

Landry walked to the back of the room and stood before the barred door. Thwarted yesterday, he racked his brain now to come up with an idea how to get past it. When he grabbed the bars and shook them forcefully, the door swung open, and he fell backward, landing hard on the floor.

He hoisted himself up and stood before the open gate. What the hell was this about? This time all it had taken was a pull, because the damn thing was unlocked. Now he had to get through the wooden door just behind the barred gate.

Is it locked? If so, should I break it down?

In the furthest corner of the vault where the

candlelight didn't reach, the old man wearing an Astros ball cap fingered the straps on his bib overalls as he watched Landry work.

CHAPTER THIRTY

The flimsy door was locked, but two firm kicks remedied that minor inconvenience, and Landry entered a room half the size of the main vault. He played the light stick in all directions: a high-top table and tall chairs stood in the middle, and the walls were lined with cabinets of varying sizes. Some held drawers, some were traditional file cabinets, and others had what looked like doors to broom closets. In the back was a set of oversized double doors. Nothing had locks; he figured this deep inside a "vault within a vault" there was no need for further security.

Some of the drawers were labeled—Teller 1, Teller 2 and so forth. He opened one and saw a typical removable till, its slots filled with bills and coins, with a tally sheet lying on top that had been signed off by the head cashier on September 3, 1935, at 2:15 p.m. This till belonged to one of the women lying dead in the other room, and Nancy Stallings, who wrote the journal, had affixed her signature confirming the count.

He picked up a few bills and saw how different they looked from the currency of today. The coins were different too—buffalo nickels, Mercury head dimes, standing Liberty quarters and halves, and lots of silver dollars. An adjacent cabinet held cloth bags of coins, marked on the outside *$1000 quarters* or *$500 dollars* or *$50 cents.* Landry knew the numismatic value of this cache would be far greater than its face value.

He realized the gleam from the other room had disappeared, which meant the candle had blown out, and he felt a sudden nauseous wave of claustrophobia.

I need to get out of here fast! He heard a noise and directed his light across the room to see the barred door slowly swinging shut. He panicked, dropped the light, flew toward the door and crashed into it a moment too late. It closed with a solid click, and his heart jumped. Surely…surely it was still unlocked, but it wouldn't budge.

Who closed it? Not the wind, there's no breeze this deep in the vault, and the door's too heavy for that anyway. Hey! Hey! Is anybody out there? He directed his light through the bars but saw nothing moving.

Fear gripped him, his throat constricted, his breath came in short gasps as he began to hyperventilate, and he told himself things would be all right. He might be locked in, but he could see into the next room where the vault door remained ajar. He pushed, he jiggled, he beat with his fists, but nothing worked. He could see the darkened main vault through the bars, but he was trapped. It was time to do what he should have done earlier—get Phil and Henri involved. He pulled out his cellphone.

Inside a room sealed within a solid brick vault, it should have come as little surprise not to have cell service, but instead he began to panic. Always the levelheaded ghost hunter, he found himself petrified being locked up in a spooky vault in a spooky town full of unexplained phenomena. Again he panicked, and again he talked himself down; in a few hours, when he failed to show for breakfast and they found the Jeep missing, the guys would come and find him. At least he still had light, and to keep his mind occupied for the next few hours, he would look through the drawers and files and closets in the room.

Rows of cabinets held customer files in alphabetical order. He glanced through one and saw business loan documents. Another held a house mortgage for $1,500 and the customer's financial statements. These were the bank's most important papers, secured the best way they could in an age before digital scanning.

Landry walked to the large double doors in back; as he reached to open one, he heard a noise—a shuffling sound like someone was walking in the other room. He doused the light, ducked behind the table, and listened.

Seconds later, the overhead lights in both vaults came on, the glare momentarily blinding Landry. As he struggled to focus, he thought he saw a figure standing outside the barred door. He rubbed his eyes and looked again.

How is this possible? As he realized it wasn't possible at all, a sharp pang of fear shot through his brain. As real as the man appeared, Landry knew nothing was as it seemed, because this couldn't be happening.

"Landry, are you okay? Are you hurt?"

He stood and took a few steps forward. He saw, but he didn't understand. "Who are you? How can the lights be on? There hasn't been electricity in this town for years. Who are you?"

"It's me, Landry. It's Jack, remember? Your friend Jack Blair from New Orleans. I thought you'd be glad to see me. Did you hit your head or something?"

I didn't hit anything, and one thing's certain. No matter how much you look and sound and act like Jack Blair, that's not who you are.

"Get me out of here."

The man pulled the bars open. "It's unlocked. You can come out."

Landry crossed through into the main vault, but when the figure reached out to hug him, he pulled back. "Tell me how the lights came on. And tell me who you are."

This time the voice was different—deeper in tone and tinged with a snide air of superiority. "You're a smart man, Landry Drake. You know the lights aren't really on. That's physically impossible, right? As you pointed out, there's no power here. I did that. I wanted them on, so they came on. As far as who I am, that answer lies somewhere deep in your brain. You've seen me before in other paranormal situations you investigated, and now we meet in person."

As he tried to make sense of it, Landry struggled to remain calm and remember why he was here. "Where is Jack? What have you done with him?"

"He's alive, if that gives you consolation. Whether he remains so is up to you."

"I want to see him."

"If you want to see him, all you need do is look at my face. It's his face."

"But you're not Jack. I want to see him."

"Is this what you're looking for?"

The face that had been Jack's began to melt. From everywhere—his brow, cheeks, chin—droplets of flesh-colored moisture dripped onto the floor. The eyes became orbs of brightness lit by tiny flames. Within seconds his friend's face was replaced by an underlay of pockmarks and scars and two lips pulled tight into a perpetual sneer. Jagged, yellowed teeth gleamed like fangs in the light.

It was then that the lights went out, shrouding the room in inky blackness. He waited a moment, listening, before clicking on his light stick. He was alone, thank God. He ran into the street, jumped into the Jeep, and raced toward the archway. As he careened through it, his phone rang.

Jack Blair.

Keeping one hand on the wheel to steer onto the narrow lane that led back to civilization, he pressed the speaker. "Jack, is that you?"

"I know that you came to find me, Landry. I can't thank you enough."

"I…I didn't do anything…"

"Oh yes, you did. Thanks to you, I'm free."

"Free? Where are you? I'll come back…"

"There's no need to do that. I'm sitting in the back seat right behind you."

He shouted, and his hands clinched the wheel. He peered into the rearview mirror, saw no one, and turned to look over his shoulder, jerking the steering wheel to the right and losing control of the Wrangler. It slid down a slope, and as its front wheel hit the water, the vehicle tilted at a steep angle. The front bumper slammed into a mangrove tree, Landry was thrown forward, and his head hit the steering wheel. The last thing he remembered was wondering if somebody was in the back seat.

CHAPTER THIRTY-ONE

As Landry knew they would, Henri and Phil came to Midnight Pass as soon as they realized both he and the Jeep weren't at the B&B. Unable to reach him by cellphone and absent a vehicle, they walked to city hall, explained their concern, and convinced Chief Hawkins to drive them.

They left the chief's big Tahoe at the barricade and walked almost a mile down the narrow lane until they saw the disabled Jeep skewed awkwardly where it had veered off the path. They found him still behind the wheel, trapped by a seat belt that wouldn't unlock. His phone lay in the grass next to the Jeep, just out of reach. He explained away the accident as having been distracted, but as Chief Hawkins walked back to his SUV to get cutters, Landry told Henri and Phil the real reason his Jeep was stuck—thinking somebody was in the back seat. As it turned out, no one was there, but the call was real—it still appeared in his call list—and he apologized for inconveniencing everyone.

In a moment they heard the truck approach. The chief brought it in close enough to hook the Jeep's winch to his bumper, and in a few minutes they had the rented Wrangler back on track. He thanked the chief, but as he began to explain why he'd come last night and what had happened, Hawkins waved him off, saying, "I've got a full calendar today. Glad I could help, but I'll see you guys back in town sometime." With that, he backed around and left.

"I think we're wearing out our welcome," Henri commented. "Let's go back to Midnight Pass, you tell us what happened during the night, and we'll plan our day accordingly." That idea got thwarted within an hour, via a phone call to Landry from New Orleans. "It's Cate," he said when the call came. "She called a bunch of times while I was trapped by the seat belt, but there was nothing I could do."

Henri smiled. "I've never been married, so this is just an observation. You might have called her back the moment you got free."

He answered. "Hi, Cate. Sorry about that. Long story, but I couldn't get to my phone until now."

"Hey, it's nice to hear from you. How about that pact we have to stay in touch?" She was angry, rightfully so, he conceded, and he admitted he'd been preoccupied with finding Jack. "There's been a lot going on," he added, which did nothing to ease the tension.

"I finished the books for the month yesterday afternoon. I'm sorry about Jack, and I understand your concern, but we have to move on. You've spent too much time and energy on this—money too, I might add—and it's time to leave the search to the professionals. You all have to come back and get to work."

You don't understand. The professionals aren't doing anything. "Just a few more days," he offered, but she shut him down. "Tomorrow. I've booked three seats on the morning flight from Fort Myers. I'll pick you up at the airport. And tell Henri his missing crates are back here in the office. The airline delivered them yesterday."

There was no use arguing. She was right; despite the paranormal manifestations, he hadn't seen or heard from the real Jack Blair since he arrived. Someone…or something…was running this supernatural carnival at Midnight Pass, and they'd gotten enough footage to create a mini-episode he could use as a backdrop to the catastrophe on Labor Day 1935. Sadly, they'd lost footage too—important evidence Phil captured that had disappeared in minutes—but nowhere had they found hard evidence to prove Jack had ever been there.

After hearing all about Landry's harrowing night in the vault, they spent the afternoon packing Henri's equipment and loading it into the U-Haul trailer. That evening they had a farewell dinner at the Chokoloskee dive bar that even Henri had come to enjoy, and afterwards they sat around the pool. Beers in hand—the rest of the fine French burgundy in Henri's—they toasted Jack, promised to keep trying to find him, and turned in early. It was over an hour to the airport, and with the cargo to check, they'd meet in the lobby, packed and ready at six.

———

Landry's summons back to Midnight Pass came in the form of another dream, a scene from his childhood—kids playing on seesaws, swings and merry-go-rounds, under the watchful eyes of Mrs. Parsons, Mrs. Huff and Miss Goddard. He and his friend Doug hoisted themselves up onto the monkey bars, navigated the crossbars from one end to the other, then dropped to the ground and ran on a collision course toward a group of girls, veering at the last minute and laughing as they screamed.

Saint Charles Street Elementary School in Jeanerette, Louisiana, was the setting for what Landry had begun calling the dream of the week, a frustratingly predictable occurrence since the ordeal at Midnight Pass had begun. The settings were always places that had nothing to do with the town, but every dream contained one bizarre situation that linked the two. In this one, it happened when the bell rang, recess was over, and everyone began running back into the school building. Just as Landry reached the steps, he heard someone call his name.

Landry. Landry. Over here!

Eleven-year-old Landry Drake turned and saw a man standing outside the chain-link fence that ringed the playground. Although he would not meet Jack Blair for many years, Landry both recognized him and knew he needed Landry's help. He stared at the man until Miss Goddard took his arm and said, "Go on in now, Landry. You're going to be tardy if you don't get a move on."

Just as he entered his old grade school, Landry awoke, sat up and stared blankly around the room. The clock beside his bed read 5:17 a.m., and the plan was to meet Phil and Henri in the lobby at six. While he showered, he thought about what he'd say to Chief Hawkins when he went to see him this morning, because one thing was certain—he couldn't go back to New Orleans with things in limbo like this.

In the days since Jack had gone missing, the authorities had unearthed no clues. The mysterious video that showed the destruction of Midnight Pass, the dreams and Landry's paranormal experiences—all were met either with skepticism, as in the case of the Monroe and Collier County sheriff departments, or with bewilderment—as was the situation with the police chief in Everglades City. Chief Hawkins wanted to believe, but pragmatism was what drove law enforcement.

Show me the facts. Give me hard evidence. Point me to a clue—any clue that doesn't involve spirits, dreams and flashbacks. If I'm going to help, I must have something to show people who deal in cold, hard evidence.

So far those had been things Landry couldn't provide.

He and the chief had had some frank conversations. He was a confirmed fan, saying he never missed one of Landry's supernatural episodes, but he didn't think any of them were real. Ghostly hauntings in ancient mansions, mysterious cults in the Louisiana bayous, a deadly red serpent and a ritual in a Savannah ballroom—it all made for spine-tingling entertainment, the same as a great horror flick left you both sweating in fear and clamoring for more.

Many of Landry's viewers believed the same, he and the Paranormal Network crew knew it, but that didn't dissuade them from searching for new material. What mattered to Landry was ensuring the episodes *were* real. There were plenty of unexplained phenomena; his job was to weed out the fakes and go after the truth.

After watching Landry at work in Midnight Pass, Chief Hawkins admitted he was a converted believer, adding, "Given all that happened there, how could it not be haunted?" But as much as he believed and wanted to help, he couldn't afford to go around blaming everything on the supernatural. He was still the head cop in a little town filled with levelheaded, pragmatic citizens.

Landry got it; the chief would be laughed out of town if folks learned he was using the paranormal to search for a missing person. But things had happened that couldn't be explained away. Something frightening was happening in Midnight Pass, and Hawkins knew it. He had promised to keep helping Landry look for his missing friend as long as he could. So this morning before he went south, Landry wanted to talk to the chief once more. Time was short, and resources were running out.

———

Henri and Phil snagged coffees from the restaurant and were surprised when Landry walked into the lobby dressed in shorts and a T-shirt. "I'm not going," he announced. "Cate will understand; if she doesn't, then I'll make it up to her somehow. There's a piece of this I'm missing, and I can't abandon Jack without one last try. I was up all night wrestling with it. I'm better equipped to deal with the paranormal than anyone, and I'm Jack's last hope. I'll tell Cate I'm on the same flight tomorrow. Now get out of here before I start crying."

His quip broke the solemnity of the moment, and they all burst out laughing. They understood what he had to do, and he hoped he could make her understand too. She'd be angry, but she couldn't argue his loyalty and friendship.

"With all the activity down there, I'm worried about leaving you," Henri admitted, "but I'm not surprised either." Phil advised him to use his cellphone to record anything else that looked interesting, and after one bear hug, they walked to the Jeep.

"Don't get yourself in trouble," Phil yelled out the window as they drove away. "That would piss Cate off for sure."

PART FOUR

THE INHABITANT

CHAPTER THIRTY-TWO

Ed Hawkins was Landry's last hope. He could expect no help from the sheriffs of Collier and Monroe Counties unless he could prove that a modern-day, flesh-and-blood criminal was the perpetrator. Landry's reputation as a famous TV ghost hunter was a negative to these men who refused to consider that the paranormal might exist. Although he believed, it was the same with Chief Hawkins—the fear of ridicule was a powerful reason to keep one's thoughts and beliefs to oneself.

The affable proprietor of the Ivey House, who'd insisted on updates about Landry's adventures in Midnight Pass, lent him an old pickup truck for the remaining time he'd be around, and after his friends left, Landry drove to city hall.

After pulling the Jeep out of the swamp yesterday, the chief left abruptly as if something was wrong. Landry had pushed him enough; all he intended to do this morning was to thank him again and say goodbye.

Today Chief Hawkins couldn't have been more different. He offered coffee, ushered Landry into his office, and closed the door. "I apologize for being so curt yesterday. I've had a lot on my mind, and Midnight Pass isn't even my jurisdiction, but it's all I can think about. I'd like to ask you a question that maybe you'll answer and maybe you won't. You're an expert at this supernatural stuff. In your opinion, what really is going on down there?"

Having wrestled with this enigma since he arrived, Landry paused to gather his thoughts. There was so much going on in so many ways, that wrapping it into a simple answer was impossible. He began by explaining how high energy levels associated with tragedies, powerful forces at work or unexplainable phenomena frequently spawned paranormal manifestations. How and why, no one knew for sure, but he'd seen it many times. And Midnight Pass was the grandfather of all tragedies. The death of a town and every living soul in it had generated an energy force so palpable Landry could feel it as he walked the streets.

A few people going missing in the Everglades over decades could be dismissed as coincidence, but recently there had been three in as many weeks—first a couple, then Jack. None seemed to have disappeared on purpose; they left behind jobs and lives, unfinished business and loose ends. So what was the common thread in the seven who had gone missing since 1988, and had there been others earlier?

One common phenomenon involved crumbling buildings that morphed into intact, well-kept structures that were memories from the beholder's past. Those impossible events were somehow so real that Phil had even managed to record one. They triggered emotions and memories, but Landry couldn't explain why they happened.

He told Chief Hawkins about his experience in the bank vault the night before last. It was the first time he had evidence that a person—or something appearing as one—was behind the strange occurrences. From the moment he saw Jack, Landry knew it wasn't him. When he called foul, the creature dropped the facade, revealing a countenance that resembled a gory Halloween mask. What the reason for that was, Landry didn't know.

He had been distracted by Jack's voice from the back of the Jeep and gone off the road. It wasn't him, of course, but if he'd tumbled into the swamp, he could have been killed. Was his demise the purpose behind the goings-on at Midnight Pass? If so, who was pulling the strings, and why hadn't they used the ample opportunities to make it happen already?

"I'm sorry to have dumped on you like this," Landry said as Chief Hawkins poured him another cup of coffee. "I guess I needed to talk out everything, and your question opened the floodgates."

The chief said, "After my bailing on you yesterday, there's no need for an apology. If I wasn't interested in your thoughts, I wouldn't have asked. When we first met, I told you I was afraid of Midnight Pass because I got bad vibes when my friend and I went there. I've been back a couple of times with you, and it still gives me the creeps. Can places be bad, Landry? Because in my opinion, that is one bad place."

Landry explained a little about what he thought. While exploring the paranormal, he had gone to frightening physical locations—an old insane asylum, more than one haunted mansion, a children's nursery filled with horrors, and more—but he believed it was never the building that created the manifestations. Entities—spirits, angels, demons and the like—and sometimes living people were always the cause behind the effect. Whether it was for gain or spite or something else, eventually Landry had been able to ferret out the reasons.

Here, he'd been stymied so far, and he had less than twenty-four hours remaining. A mission that had been about finding Jack now included him as well. With every visit he became more certain he was being drawn into something evil, but if he didn't go back, he'd never find the answers.

After spending nearly an hour, Landry rose to go and learned for the first time that Chief Hawkins actually did have other things on his plate, just as he'd said yesterday. One of the airboat drivers who hauled tourists through the Everglades had come upon a cache of drugs hidden in mangrove roots just south of town. State narcotics agents were already on the scene, and Hawkins had one of the biggest cases his little town had seen in decades. Landry thanked him for giving him time he didn't have to spare, and the chief said he'd enjoyed getting to know Landry in the short time he'd been there.

"I've told you how much Midnight Pass freaks me out, but I'd go with you right now if I could arrange it," he said sincerely as Landry stood outside his office. "I'm sorry I don't have time to work with you. Keep me advised about what you're doing and call me if you get into trouble. I'll send help if you need it."

CHAPTER THIRTY-THREE

Not long ago, Luce Moros had laughed aloud when he learned the highly rated podcast *Travel Dog* warned tourists against going to Midnight Pass. Bad things happened there—eerie stuff you couldn't explain away. Luce had never listened to a podcast, but he had a sixth sense that gave him knowledge of things that mattered.

People didn't come often, but now and then someone ventured onto what once had been a road that headed off into the swamps and dead-ended in Midnight Pass. The sound of a car engine in the distance, maybe a lost soul or an adventurer following the rutted lane to see where it went, excited Luce. The times when a person ventured through the fence into the town itself Luce called his lucky days. The people who arrived in his town, not so much.

Warnings only serve to deter the meek, he thought. The brave considered danger a challenge, and that kept them coming. The paranormal investigator Landry Drake was different; he returned over and over, whetting his insatiable appetite for the supernatural, and Luce was more than willing to dish it out.

He walked down streets past crumbling buildings that once housed a vaudeville theater, hotel, saloon, drugstore, church and the other enterprises that support a town. Nowadays each rotting edifice had its own subset of issues. At midnight a church bell rang twelve times, tolling the hour. He loved to stroll through town in the darkness, viewing the crumbled facades, the dark, empty windows, walking past the spots where each of 162 people died in a hurricane. These things made Midnight Pass unique; no other community on earth had suffered like this one. The man knew it by heart; he had been in Midnight Pass for a very, very long time—not *living* here, but inhabiting it. The difference was more than semantics, because the man wasn't capable of *living* anywhere.

Luce Moros, whose name was neither Luce—a sobriquet he created—nor Moros, the surname he adopted when necessary, turned on Second Street and passed the ruins of the King of Kings Catholic Church. The bell that had just pealed throughout the quiet town lay in a heap of rubble where it had fallen when the 1935 hurricane destroyed the church. It hadn't rung in eighty-seven years, but Luce had a way of making things happen when it suited him.

He took a deep breath of humid air and salivated at the challenges tomorrow would bring. The anticipation always enthused him, but this time things would be completely different. In the morning Landry Drake would return to find his lost friend and unearth the secrets of Midnight Pass. He was different from the others—the accidental visitors, the curious and the adventuresome. Those had no agendas, no intention of debunking mysteries. Circumstance brought them—getting lost, or poking around a ghost town, or visiting a scene captured in a moment in time. A change in tactics would be required for tomorrow's formidable paranormal investigator.

Luce hadn't faced a challenge in ages, and his skin bristled with excitement. *This one may be crafty, but you have the upper hand. Don't play all your cards at once, and don't let anticipation cause you to miss the satisfaction of success.* After tomorrow, the ghost hunter would leave Midnight Pass, so it was time to set the hook that would get Luce the prize he wanted. He savored a challenge; there were none these days as the world went about its business bombing and hating and killing. All was well, and he relished the confrontation that would come in the morning. The streets of Midnight Pass would once again be alive, as the one who knew the secrets faced off against the man who wanted answers.

CHAPTER THIRTY-FOUR

The ancient pickup Landry borrowed wouldn't have made it down the narrow lane, so he left it at the barricade, donned his backpack, and hiked in. The morning was beautiful, cicadas in the mangroves buzzed, birds soared overhead, and the occasional splash in the nearby swamp reminded him to stay in the middle of the path. As always, the moment he walked through the gate, the weather changed. Tendrils of fog draped the shells that lined the streets, and an oppressive gloom permeated the town.

Today he'd finish exploring the two rooms inside the bank vault to see if those final survivors of the hurricane had left any other information that might prove useful. To ensure he wouldn't be trapped like before, he stacked debris to block open both the large round door and the smaller barred one inside. He flicked on the light stick and entered.

After an hour poring through the bank's file cabinets and records, he opened each of the many drawers, finding a great deal more coins and currency than before. He made a mental note to tell Chief Hawkins that someone should come get this hoard of numismatic valuables before anyone discovered it. He worked his way back until he came to the set of wooden double cabinet doors. They were secured by a simple hasp and no lock, and as he reached to unsnap it, he heard a voice.

"Don't do it."

He whirled around and cried, "Jack!" before catching himself. "Is it really you?" he said, and the figure nodded. "After what happened to me in the bank vault, I want proof. How can I be sure?"

"It's me, Landry. Listen to my voice, watch my facial expressions, pinch my arm—do anything you want. The person you saw in the vault wasn't me, but now I'm here. And I'm warning you, don't open those doors."

"Prove it. Tell me something only you would know."

"Ask me anything. How we met on Toulouse Street in the French Quarter. What kind of soda I drank back then. What the name of our station manager is. Ask away."

Landry thought a moment. "Remember that time we used hypnosis to regress you to a previous life?"

"Sure. What about it?"

"In that previous life, what was your name?"

"Lucas LaPiere. I was the owner of the building where your Paranormal Network studio is today."

"Okay, one more. What were you doing, and what was I doing, when we first met?"

"You were on a ghost tour of the Quarter, and I was living in a box in a recessed area outside a vacant building."

That was enough to convince Landry. Maybe an entity could have known the answers, but he was willing to accept Jack. He ran to him, and they hugged like brothers. "Where have you been?" he asked.

"You'll find this hard to believe, but I've been here in Midnight Pass all along, in my childhood bedroom in Memphis."

"In that house where we saw you playing ball as a kid? That's impossible."

"There's just so much you don't…I should say you *can't* understand. I don't even know how to begin."

"Begin by telling me what happened to you. You vanished—did he…did someone kidnap you?"

"Technically, I guess. I can't leave, so yeah, I'm sort of a prisoner here."

"What are you talking about? What's stopping you from walking out with me right now?"

"I can't. I'm part of something now. You don't understand…"

"Stop telling me that, dammit! Why don't you just explain it to me?"

"He took me because he knew you'd come here to find me."

"Who? Who took you?"

"I'm not sure. He calls himself Luce…"

"Talk to me, Jack! Is he real, or is he something supernatural?"

"He's real enough, but he's definitely supernatural. Everything happening here is about you, Landry, and even what you see with your own eyes may not be real. I'm on your side; keep that in mind no matter what. He wants to trap you, the person he considers his nemesis as a paranormal investigator. He considers what you do as prying into his business."

"Prying? I investigate—I do television documentaries. That's not prying."

"According to Luce, it is. You bring too much attention to the paranormal. He prefers to work in the shadows."

Jack pulled something from his pocket and handed it over. "Here, take this. You'll need it."

Landry looked at a fresh deck of playing cards still sealed in cellophane. "Why are you giving me this?"

"Because you'll need them; it's all going to come down to a card game. If he furnished the deck, I guarantee you'd lose. Even with a fair deck, I doubt you can win against him…but then of all people, maybe Landry Drake can. Here are a few suggestions, for what they're worth. I've only used the first one, but this is what I've observed. Pray. Evidence your faith and pray in front of him because it sends him into a frenzy. Stand up to him too; confrontation bewilders him because everyone's afraid of him. Be strong, and don't cut him any slack."

Jack's nonchalance confounded Landry. His conversation about a monumental battle—the showdown between good and evil—flowed as easily and effortlessly as if he were teaching a child how to play Monopoly. Landry said, "You seem resigned to all this, as though you're on his side and I have no chance of winning. You already told me you can't leave. Eventually he'll get me too. When this is over, he'll have us both. You understand that, right? And you understand why somehow, in some way we have to beat him? If not, he'll never let us go."

"It is what it is, and if that means I'm resigned, then I am. As to whether he'll let me go in the end, that depends on you, I guess. Like I said, you've been digging into unexplainable things and showing the world the supernatural exists for years, far too long, according to him. I guess it was bound to catch up with you sometime. I'm just the cheese in the trap that brought you here."

What? "It was bound to catch up with me? What the hell are you talking about? Come on, Jack. Has he brainwashed you or something? Help me understand this."

He shook his head. "Believe me, I wish I could. All I can tell you is what I said before. You're going to play a game for all the marbles, one where you put it all on the line."

"So that's all the answer I get? You refuse to help me, so how about telling me what's behind those double doors that's such a damned big deal?" He pointed to the back wall of the smaller cash vault, which he'd been ready to open a moment ago before Jack had cautioned him not to.

"You don't want to do that, Landry. Please. Please trust me. Some things in Midnight Pass are better left alone."

Landry was aghast. He'd given Jack a hand, picked him up, fed and housed him, gotten him a job, and ended up with a recovery case that made everyone proud, Jack most of all. Now Jack had an interesting job in broadcasting, a girlfriend and a bright future. Landry didn't want his praise or thanks, it had been due to Jack's own determination that he succeeded, but here and now, he wanted answers from a man—his supposed friend—who seemed unconcerned about the whole situation. His flippant, carefree attitude was an enigma…and it pissed Landry off.

"If it's really you I'm talking to, then you can go to hell, Jack. Watch this." He walked to the back, removed the hasp and pulled the double doors wide open. As he looked inside, speechless and light-headed, he mumbled unintelligible syllables and lifted a finger to point.

"Wha…wha the…aah…oh God…"

"I tried to warn you," Jack murmured before walking out of the vault, leaving Landry to confront the horror alone.

CHAPTER THIRTY-FIVE

Not since the bizarre beheadings in an old mansion called Proctor Hall had Landry viewed something like this. He stared, mesmerized and somehow unable to avert his eyes as his brain struggled to process the meaning of the shocking, grotesque display. This was horror in its rawest form—a collage or a collection, perhaps, but surely the creation of someone utterly devoid of mercy and sanity.

With its row of hooks along the back, the tall cabinet resembled a coat closet, although this one had been repurposed in a grisly manner. There were thirteen cadavers, male and female, younger and older, each hanging from its own hook, and on the far right end were two empty hooks. Next to each was a printed card tacked to the wall. The bodies increasingly decomposed as one looked from left to right, but thanks to the lack of air in the vault, they were in a remarkably good state of preservation. A light dusting of gray powder—mold, Landry figured—covered their faces, as had been the case with the victims in the outer vault.

Landry wondered if the cards would explain the purpose of this cabinet of horrors, and he took a few steps closer to look. The first body on the left was an adult male wearing a cowboy hat and boots. *Franklin Duvall, January 1937,* read the card. Next were two teenaged girls who had on bright sundresses. *Betty Ferguson, 1949. Millie Cross, 1949.*

Realizing what the cards signified, he moved to the other end to confirm his suspicions. *Grant Stark, 2022. Shannon Black, 2022.* These two wore T-shirts, shorts and hiking boots, and Landry took an involuntary step back, gasping as he saw their fresh, ruddy faces and blank stares. He recognized the names, and now he understood. These were the campers who'd most recently vanished in Midnight Pass, and this double-door cabinet was someone's trophy case, and they were arranged in date order from left to right.

Bile began to rise in his throat, and he struggled to keep from vomiting. What kind of warped mind would it take to showcase the people he murdered?

Beginning in 1988 and not including Jack, six people had disappeared in Midnight Pass. But the sight before Landry filled in a missing piece. Now he knew there had really been thirteen, beginning in 1937, two years after the Labor Day Hurricane. A serial killer had been at work all these years…but this stalker couldn't be human. The first abduction happened eighty-five years ago; unless the killer passed his legacy down through the generations, a theory that was as bizarre as the trophy cabinet itself, this was not the work of a man.

He remembered the two empty hooks on his right and glanced at them. A wave of light-headedness swept over him, and he grabbed the wall so he wouldn't collapse. He read the neatly printed cards. *Jack Blair, 2022. Landry Drake, 2022.*

Now two things were certain—the man called Luce would never free Jack, nor did Luce intend to lose the game.

CHAPTER THIRTY-SIX

"Jack! Jack, where are you?" Landry shouted as he walked down the gloomy streets. A sharp streak of lightning pierced the dark clouds, followed by a low growl of thunder and the first pitter-pat of raindrops. Within minutes the shower became a full-fledged storm as windswept rain hammered the crumbling structures and turned the streets into mud pits. Oblivious, Landry went block by block, shouting for his friend, although even if Jack had answered, his words would have gone unheard in the screeching, howling wind.

Drenched to the bone, he kept going, struggling to answer the pressing questions. A trophy case—that was what it was, just like the one in the hall at his high school, where they had displayed the intramural awards and championship rings. The perpetrator who'd gotten away with so many kidnappings over the years displayed them in a cabinet, but for what purpose? To come view his handiwork whenever he wished? As a shrine of some kind, or a place to bring his next victim and reveal the hook that was intended for them?

His extensive background as a paranormal investigator made it easier to believe the perpetrator wasn't human. Where people like Sheriff Warner and Chief Hawkins limited their thinking to common sense and logical explanations, he knew better. He and his crew had seen the supernatural in play time and again, and now he knew Midnight Pass truly was the devil's workshop. He remembered what the old-timers said. *The devil rode the hurricane into Midnight Pass that day and slaughtered every living soul. That's why Midnight Pass isn't in Florida. It's in hell.*" That cabinet bore witness to their claim.

He came to an intersection, realized he was soaked, and looked for shelter. The choices were few; only one structure in the entire town had a roof—the bank vault, a place to which Landry had no interest in returning. Facing a fifteen-minute hike back to the truck, he decided to get under the nearest tree. As he ran toward one, a flash of color caught his eye.

Landry's only personal encounter with the regressions that happened frequently in this town had been his dream about the sheriff's office in New Iberia. It had been so real, but when he stepped outside, he was in Midnight Pass, not Louisiana. He remembered that dream as he watched both sides of the block metamorphose from piles of debris to neat cottages, each with a freshly mowed lawn and a white picket fence. The dull, drab blacks and grays now were bright colors, and the sun shone down on a paved street. This was another place and one Landry knew very well. This was his street, and two doors down was the house where he grew up in Jeanerette, Louisiana.

A horn honked, and he jumped out of the way as a Chevy from the 1980s passed, a hand waving out the window. *Dad! That's my dad's car, and it's him! Dad's home!* He broke out in a run toward his house as the car pulled into the driveway.

Dad hadn't been home since 1998. Landry had been eight when his father died from cancer, and afterwards, times had been hard for him and his mother. Knowing all this couldn't be real because he was in Midnight Pass, Florida, in the year 2022, he cast all logic aside and hugged his father as hard as he could. He had to look up into his face—in that short run, he'd become a kid again, and his father laughed at Landry's exuberance as he hugged back, saying it was nice to be missed, but he'd only been gone since this morning.

You've been gone twenty-four years, Dad. I haven't hugged you in twenty-four years.

"Come on, son. I'll bet your mom's got a casserole in the oven, and we don't want to keep the old girl waiting!"

That's what you called her—the old girl—even though neither of you was as old as I am today.

His mother's voice rang out. "Landry, you wipe your feet. Larry, your father's home."

Larry! My brother, four years older than me. He dared me to go in that old insane asylum in Victory when I was fourteen. Guess that part hasn't happened yet, since Dad died when I was eight.

When Larry bounded into the room, Landry hugged him too, and Larry reacted in typical brotherly fashion. "Eew! Get away, slime bag! What the hell…"

"You watch your mouth, buster." Mom was the disciplinarian. Larry apologized, and Landry backed off, staring at the brother he hadn't seen in seven years. Larry was dead too, of course, from a car wreck that had happened when Landry was twenty-five.

Don't think about it! Just savor the moment and take it all in. Here we are—the Drake family of Jeanerette, Louisiana—in our little house on our street, with our old Chevrolet in the driveway. Smell that apple pie in the oven? Mom made it, and it's gonna be delicious!

As if someone hit the pause button, the scene froze. Mom with the hot pads, bending slightly to open the oven door. Dad looking at the headlines in the evening paper. Larry inside the fridge, getting a Dr Pepper.

"Idyllic, isn't it? You must enjoy all those memories." A man walked in from the den. He wore a black jogging suit, crimson running shoes, and sported a fancy Rolex on his arm.

Landry wasn't surprised. "I suppose it's about time we met. I was wondering when it would happen."

"I hated to interrupt your reverie. You were having so much fun seeing your dead brother and father."

"That's a kind way to describe it. So how about we cut the small talk and you tell me why all this is happening."

"Come outside with me," the man said. "I find explanations better with visuals."

They stepped out the front door and back into the gloomy fog of Midnight Pass. Behind him, his house…their block…his family had all vanished, but it didn't faze Landry because this trip down memory lane had only existed in his mind. It was time to get the questions answered.

"Are you Luce?"

"Now and then. It's a sobriquet I coined. Like my last name, Moros. Neither are real."

"Your last name's Morris?"

"*Moros*, like the Greek God of impending doom. I use it when necessary because it seems appropriate."

"Why make up a name? Are you ashamed of your own?"

The man smiled. "Patience, Mr. Drake. I assure you before this day ends, you'll know everything and more. Now let me talk with you about the visions people have in Midnight Pass. You've been privy to some since you began prying around in town. Familiar stores and houses from the past. People too, like your family. If I desire it, everybody who comes here sees memories."

"Including the thirteen people hanging in your trophy case?"

He roared with laughter. "Is that what you call it? I hadn't thought of it in that way, but I believe you have coined an appropriate description. Now where was I? As you have observed and even captured on video, I have the capacity to create certain visions. Would you like to see something truly special?"

"I'm not really in the mood for your tricks. I want answers."

Ignoring him, the man called Luce raised his hands into the air and waved them about. In seconds a scene unfolded that even Landry had to admit was something spectacular. Instead of what they'd experienced before—a fresh building sandwiched between ruined ones—the entire town, block after block, came alive.

"Walk with me," Luce said. Although the sky was gray and overcast, people were out in the streets, row after row of houses stood anew, and Landry saw the church, stores of all types and even the bank, open for business and draped in red, white and blue streamers. A large banner stretched across the main street read *Labor Day Celebration! September 3, 10:00–4:00. Meet at the bandstand!*

It was Labor Day 1935, and it appeared as though the entire town had turned out. "A hurricane's moving this way," Landry said. "Why are they celebrating instead of preparing for the storm?"

"Because they think all that's coming is a decent rainstorm," Luce explained. The people had been deceived; the weather reports they heard on their radios said the storm was a hundred miles west and moving away in the Gulf. As far as they knew, Midnight Pass would get some rain, but the brunt of the storm would be far away. A few residents had left, but of the hundred and sixty-two remaining, most were out in the town square this morning.

"They got false weather reports," Landry said. "I'm guessing those came from you."

The man smiled and nodded.

"Why? What had these people ever done to you?"

"These people? Nothing, really. They did bother me a bit; they were irritating Bible-thumping Christians spouting scripture like a gushing fountain, going to church Wednesday night and twice on Sunday. I got tired of it, that's all. I just wanted to stir things up a little."

"You haven't had much use for Christians for a long, long time. What is it about believing in Jesus that you find irritating?"

He grinned. "Think you have it all figured out, Mr. Drake? I wouldn't be so sure. Come on. The band's about to play."

They walked to the square where the cremation pyre had stood, but this morning an eight-piece brass band played in an ornate gazebo. The musicians were belting out Sousa marches while onlookers sang, clapped and enjoyed ice cream and sodas bought from a vendor with a bicycle cart. It was a perfect morning in a typical small American town that was about to be obliterated off the face of the earth for no reason.

A man who could make it storm every time Landry showed up could surely have rerouted the Labor Day Hurricane away from these "Bible-thumping Christians." But that wasn't what he was after that day in 1935. He "just wanted to stir things up a little," so he'd brought it in for a direct hit.

CHAPTER THIRTY-SEVEN

"Have you finished showing off your skills?"

The man gave a slight nod, and all the newness of Midnight Pass vanished. The dark buildings and muddy streets were back. He said, "That's an admirable show of bravado, Mr. Drake, although I have a feeling you'll be groveling and begging before this day is over."

"Think *you've* got it all figured out? I wouldn't be so sure. I have another question. When I was locked in the bank vault, you were there, pretending to be Jack. You set me free when you could have let me die. Why?"

"Because I want to crush you fair and square, not trap you like an animal. What's the sport in that?"

"I see. So it's sporting to kill every adult and child in Midnight Pass. I can't imagine how much fun that must have been for you. So what do you have planned for me?"

"How about a friendly card game?"

"Do I have a chance to win?"

Luce laughed. "You're a mortal, playing against me. What do you think? But it'll be a fair game. I won't cheat, if that's what you're worried about."

"When and where?"

"High noon, just like in the cowboy movies. Two blocks north of the bank. You can't miss the place. Now, don't be late." He turned away.

"Wait a minute! What's the game, and what are the stakes?"

"Damn you and the questions. We're playing Texas Hold'em for the highest stakes imaginable. I'm looking forward to it." He raised a finger into the air and vanished.

Landry wandered the streets, recalling how much had happened here. The tragedies, the losses, the mysteries and unanswered questions coursed through his brain. And the man—the being in the shape of a man—was behind it all. Although he knew who Luce really was, he found himself strangely unable, or perhaps unwilling, to say it. If he admitted it, would anything be different? He didn't know. For now, he intended to ignore the truth, because nothing mattered anymore. In two hours he'd be playing the game of his life—and likely *for* his life.

He climbed the dune and walked out onto the beach. A cold wind whipped around him, and the water lapped at his shoes as he thought about the call he had to make and the right words to use. He struggled to think of the right words to use, the way to express his feelings and tell Cate how he felt. Overwhelmed by what he faced and the probability he wouldn't see her again, he couldn't come up with anything that sounded good enough. Out of time, he placed the call.

"Hey there. I'm glad you called. I hear you're coming home tomorrow. I should be angry, but I had a feeling you'd send the boys back alone."

"Cate, I…I just want to tell you how much I love you. I don't say those words enough…" He paused to take a deep breath.

"Landry, what's wrong? Please tell me everything's okay. Is this about Jack?"

In a way it was about Jack; he used the question as a lead-in to the difficult things he wanted to express. He left nothing out and apologized at the end for being so stubborn and for not coming home as she'd insisted. But that would have sealed Jack's fate. Now his own was at stake.

They cried out in anguish as Cate realized an old wives' tale—playing a game with the devil for one's soul—was no myth. The game would take place in half an hour in Midnight Pass. The man she loved against the master of darkness.

"Please come home," she cried when he said it was time to go. "Please don't die, Landry. Please don't. Promise me…"

"I'll do everything I can, I promise." Tears ran down his cheeks as he disconnected and stared at the phone, dazed and lost. This was twenty-first-century America. Surely such a confrontation couldn't really happen.

But he knew better. It was time to go.

CHAPTER THIRTY-EIGHT

At twenty minutes before twelve, Landry left the beach, scaled the high dune and headed back into town. He had the most important appointment of his life to keep, but he had one thing to do first. As he walked, he thought, would this be the last time he'd walk through the gate? Was this the last stroll down Main Street in a town filled with horror?

He walked a few blocks, coming to the building containing the vault and the macabre trophy case, grim testimony that even today, decades after the hurricane, visitors to Midnight Pass couldn't escape the horror. Landry wound through the rubble, stepping in familiar spots to avoid nails and rotten timbers and loose bricks, until he came to the massive door. He pulled it open, took out his light stick, and walked inside.

There would be none of the revulsion and disgust that had swept over him when he first saw the hanging corpses. Today he had a reason for confronting the dead; he wanted—he *needed* to etch each of their faces into his brain so he'd remember those in whose memories he'd be playing the game. An overwhelming sense of purpose swept through him, he would win, and he would ensure this madness ended. How, he had no idea, but the devil's trophies became the sole motivation for beating the devil at his own game. If he lost his life—his own soul—to save innocent people in the future, then it would all be worth it.

He walked to the back of the cash vault, stood before the closed double doors and said a prayer, took a deep breath, and pulled them open wide. The corpses hung in single file, and he vowed that today they would be avenged. He forced himself to spend a moment with each, staring into their empty eyes, speaking their names and dates aloud and etching them into his memory. He moved from one to another, and as he neared the end, he realized something was off. This wasn't the same—it was dreadfully different.

Today only one hook remained empty—his own.

His heart sank, and he gasped for breath as he shifted over to the next-to-last hook, now occupied, fearing and knowing what he would find. He looked slowly up into the lifeless face of Jack Blair.

"You bastard. You sneaky, conniving son of a bitch. YOU BASTARD!" His screams bounced off the walls as he beat on the doors, realizing he'd been outsmarted before the first card had been dealt. Luce had taken Jack.

"I won't let you get away with this, you damned bastard! You think you're so clever, but by God, this isn't finished yet. By God, I'm going to beat you!"

Shaking with rage, he turned to go, but he noticed something—a sliver of white protruding from Jack's shirt pocket. He reached up and removed a playing card. The ace of spades.

"Thank you, Jack," he whispered. "I don't know why you gave me this, but thank you." He paused a moment, considering the best place to hide it.

He marched in grim determination down the street and spotted the venue from two blocks away. Bright and shining among the blackened hulks, it was impossible to miss. At the top of the two-story building was a sign that read "Saloon." Four flickering gas lamps hung from a balcony, and a pair of swinging doors led into a large, noisy room. He found himself transported into the 1890s.

People—men and a few scantily dressed ladies—occupied several of the tables, playing cards, drinking and engaging in loud discussions. In a corner, a man wearing a red garter on his sleeve played honky-tonk music on an upright piano, while girls in lingerie and hose served drinks. Several people wore pistols on their belts. Landry pulled a pair of glasses from his pocket, put them on, and slammed the doors aside, striding in and surveying the room. In a moment, a server approached him.

"Where is he? Take me to the bastard."

"Come with me, Mr. Drake. He's waiting in the back room." To his surprise, no one gave him a glance as they maneuvered between tables, although his clothing was a century different than theirs. It was as though he didn't exist, but he knew the truth. In reality, it was the other way around. Like his childhood home and the sheriff's office in New Iberia, none of this was real. The only reality in Midnight Pass lay in the trophy case…and in the back room of this saloon.

She showed him to the door and opened it, stepping aside and closing it behind him. The man called Luce sat on the far side of a round felt-covered table, a shot glass filled with brown liquid and a deck of cards within arm's reach. He was dressed all in black—Stetson, pants and studded shirt.

Landry sneered, "This is all a little hokey, don't you think? I feel like I've stepped into a B-western. Next thing you know, Kenny Rogers will stroll in singing 'The Gambler.'"

"I can arrange a concert if it suits you. Sit down, Mr. Drake. Make yourself comfortable; hopefully for you, we have a long afternoon ahead. I hope so too; it makes things more interesting when the game lasts awhile. Would you care for something to drink?"

Landry took hold of a chair and flung it across the room, where it crashed into a wall and splintered. "I saw the trophy case, you bastard! This changes everything. When did you kill Jack?"

"Does it matter?"

"Nothing matters to you. Let's get a few things out in the open before we begin. I want you to tell me who you are. I think I know, because there's only one godforsaken, miserable creature on earth that could do all this, but I want to hear it from your lips. You call yourself Luce, a nickname. For what? What's your real name?"

"Names hardly matter where I come from. Some folks call me Lucifer, so I made up the nickname Luce."

"So you're the devil—the master of darkness. No surprise there, given the horror you brought down on the poor citizens of Midnight Pass. Why did you choose it? Was it really the god-fearing people that drove you to annihilate them and their town?"

"Why does my motive concern you? Accept it at face value. I gave it no thought. There was a tremendous storm, and I steered it to Midnight Pass just for the—"

"For the hell of it?" Landry snorted. "How original."

"You're not afraid, are you, Mr. Drake? You should be terrified, but I sense that you have peace about this. That seems odd; explain it to me."

"I believe in God and his power, and I reject you and all you stand for. You're as fake as this building and everyone in it. You're a sideshow huckster, a deceiver and a murderer of innocent people. I stood before each of those unfortunates a few minutes ago—including my friend Jack—and I swore to them I'd win the card game."

"I'm a fake yet a murderer of innocent people? How

can that be? What a dilemma you have! Oh well, I suppose I'll never understand you people. If you're ready, shall we begin?" He reached for the cards.

Landry brought over another chair, sat and removed Jack's deck from his pocket. "We'll play with these."

"Are you worried that I'll cheat?"

Landry rolled his eyes, broke the cellophane, and took out the deck. "That's so obvious it doesn't merit an answer. Are we still playing Texas Hold'em?"

"That's right. Best two out of three hands."

The choice of games could have been worse. Landry had played a lot of poker in high school and college, drinking beer and smoking Swisher Sweets with his buddies. He'd followed *World Series of Poker* when it was popular on network TV back in the day, and he'd held his own playing Texas Hold'em at casinos in Bossier City and New Orleans. He'd have a chance in a fair game, but even with Jack's deck of cards, he expected his opponent to cheat. He needed a strategy, help from God, and a miracle.

Landry asked the question of the day. "What does the winner get?"

He flashed a debauched grin. "It's like the scary stories you heard as a child, Mr. Drake. If I win, I get your souls."

Already struggling with his emotions, that answer gave him a shudder. The man was right—every story about the devil included his wanting people's souls. And now, as an underdog in what likely was a no-win situation, those tales could become reality here in this room.

"Souls plural? Whose souls? I saw Jack Blair hanging with the others. You already have him."

"I have his life, Mr. Drake, but as of yet I haven't taken his soul. I thought it would be interesting to allow you to gamble for his soul as well as your own."

"And if I win?"

Luce bellowed with laughter. "If you win. What an

amusing thought. I hadn't really considered it. Let's see, if you win, you walk away unscathed, leave Midnight Pass behind, and go about your life."

"That's not enough. You'll return Jack to life, you killed him, and you can bring him back. We both go free and keep our souls. You leave Midnight Pass and never come back. Nobody else gets hurt here, ever."

"Anything else? Would you also like a red Maserati? This isn't your Christmas list, Mr. Drake. You know who I am. Do you seriously consider yourself in a position to negotiate?"

Landry dropped to his knees, folded his hands together, and shouted, "Dear Lord God in Heaven, please give me the strength—"

"Enough!" Luce roared. "Get up, pathetic creature. You look like a fool on your knees talking to the air. We have a deal, Mr. Drake. If I win, I take your souls. But if you win"—he laughed heartily—"I give you and Jack your lives and souls, and I abandon Midnight Pass. I must advise you that all this negotiating is a waste of time and energy since I've never lost. Now sit down."

After Landry shuffled and dealt, the first game began.

CHAPTER THIRTY-NINE

Each player received two hole cards facedown, and then he dealt three more faceup.

Ace of hearts. Seven of diamonds. Two of spades.

Landry looked at his hole cards, a king and an eight, both diamonds. No help.

"There aren't any chips," he said. "What are we going to use to bet?"

"My mistake." Luce pointed a finger at Landry's side of the table, where a stack of chips in various colors appeared. He gave himself an equal amount and threw out a chip.

Landry didn't have a hand, but he had to call. If he folded now, he'd lose the first game. He called the bet and dealt the next card.

A four of diamonds.

Luce smiled. "Your turn to bet."

"Pass."

"Fine. I'll pass as well. Deal, Mr. Drake."

Landry dealt the remaining card faceup. The king of hearts.

Luce looked across the table at him. "Comfortable with your hand?" he asked, and Landry told him to get it over with.

"Pass." Landry passed as well, and it was time to reveal their hands. With no pairs showing, he felt reasonably comfortable that a pair of kings might win, but it was at this point he'd learn whether his opponent would play fair or not. He turned over his cards. "One pair."

Luce threw his cards on the table. "Same for me, only mine are aces. I win the first hand." He gathered the cards and began to shuffle.

That wasn't an unreasonable hand, Landry thought. Aces over kings. Not three of a kind, as he'd feared, but a simple win. Could it be that Luce was playing fair after all? Maybe on the first hand, but the next one remained to be seen.

"I have a question for you," Landry said as Luce dealt. "What about the cast of characters you introduced who weren't real, like the bird ladies and the kid on the beach and the guy Buddy Elkins from DOT. What role did they all play?"

"None, really. I was just toying with you, to see if there was any information they could learn about what you were after. No harm done."

"With all the mumbo-jumbo shit you do in Midnight Pass, I'm surprised you can't read my mind."

"Even I have limitations. Enough talk. Let's play cards."

Luce dealt the second hand. The first up cards were an eight of diamonds, a ten of hearts and a two of spades. Landry's hole cards were both jacks.

A round of betting ensued, followed by the fourth up card, the eight of clubs. Luce upped the bet this time, and Landry, holding two pairs, made a show of considering his hand carefully before calling the bet.

The last up card was a jack, giving Landry a full

house. Cautiously, he passed to see what Luce would do. He passed as well, and when the hands were revealed, Luce lost with two pairs, tens and twos.

"Nice win," he said. "Now we're even."

Landry replied, "Are you surprised, or is that the way you planned it? Did I get to win a hand so the game could play to the bitter end?"

"Whatever you think, Mr. Drake. I told you I wanted the game to last awhile. And the end will in fact be bitter for you, I'm afraid. As I said, I never lose."

The final round in the game for two human souls commenced. Landry dealt, giving himself the queen of diamonds and ten of spades. The cards lying faceup on the table were a two, a seven and the queen of spades. This was it—the deciding hand in a crucial game. Landry shuddered as he called Luce's bet and dealt the fourth up card, the jack of spades.

He considered his possibilities. He had a pair of queens, which likely wouldn't win, and he had three out of five cards to make up a royal flush—the queen, ten and jack of spades. A royal flush was the best hand of all, but the problem was that one card remained to be dealt. To make the hand, he needed two—the king and ace of spades.

But then, he really only needed one if he could retrieve the ace from his shoe without Luce noticing. He had to be casual about it, and nothing mattered anyway unless the next card dealt was the king of spades. The longest of shots, but the only hope he had.

Landry was no cheater, but if ever a situation allowed cheating, this was it. He felt certain Luce would cheat on this last hand, because of his braggadocious revelation. Any card player who never lost was a cheater. Since he was playing for his soul, he chose to believe God had provided help in the form of a playing card. Cheating the devil wouldn't be shameful, quite the opposite. It would be a victory.

"Are you a little distracted?" Luce asked, pointing to the chips he'd put in the pot. "I think you're getting nervous. I can imagine how terrifying this is, knowing you and your friend are doomed to hell. Now, are you going to call or fold?"

Landry called the bet, took a deep breath and dealt the last card, his hands shaking as he flipped it over. The king of spades. If he could pull off the switch, he had a royal flush. He crossed his leg over his knee, picked up his hole cards and made a show of examining them. He leaned over the table and looked closely at the five cards that lay faceup, removing the ace from his shoe as he held his two hole cards slightly below the tabletop. In a flash the ace was in his hand and the queen of diamonds in his shoe.

"What are you doing? Keep your cards above the table!"

"You did the same thing a minute ago. What are *you* doing? Are you cheating?"

Luce laughed. "I don't have to cheat, remember? The last card's been dealt. Do you want to make a final bet?"

"Pass."

"I'll pass as well. Now that we're finished, Mr. Drake, I'll say it's been a pleasure playing high-stakes poker with you. I must say it's more satisfying for me to have won against the famous paranormal crime-fighter than anyone I have played with in a thousand years." He laid his two hole cards faceup on the table. His hand consisted of a respectable three queens, and from the smarmy look on his face, it was clear Luce knew he'd won.

I'm cheating the devil. The thought made Landry smile as he tossed his cards out one by one. First came the ten of spades, then the ace that gave him a royal flush and the victory. He leaned back in the chair, folded his hands behind his head, and said, "Looks like I win."

CHAPTER FORTY

Luce stared blankly at the game-winning hand for a moment, smiled and said, "You cheated, Mr. Drake."

"Read 'em and weep. You lost and that's it."

"Where did that ace of spades come from? That card hasn't been in your hand."

Bingo! Landry smiled. "You cheated. You knew what my hole cards were."

"You seem so sure of yourself, so cocky and confident, but you have made a fatal error." He stood, and the body that had been Luce Moros cracked open, falling away like a shell. What emerged was a slithering reptilian centipede with fangs and horns jutting from its grotesque head. It shot up toward the ceiling, bending as it hit the rafters. Landry bolted for the door, but a scaly claw blocked his exit. Razor-sharp talons clicked inches from his face, and he lost his balance, tumbling to the ground.

"You're not going anywhere. You're going to play another hand…"

"No! It's over. You lost, I won, and it's all over." He clambered to his feet and opened the door.

"You fool! You stupid mortal fool! Do you think you can escape? There's no place you can hide I won't find you. You are dead, just like your friend Jack Blair. DEAD!"

Landry shouted, "Dear God, make your fallen angel accept his loss and do what he promised…"

The creature uttered a shriek that threatened to burst Landry's eardrums. In a flash the walls and ceiling disappeared. The rest of the saloon building fell away, and they stood in the middle of the street as a jagged streak of lightning split the ominous clouds. Landry, dwarfed by a serpent fifteen feet tall, stood his ground, relying upon the only thing in his arsenal that might keep him safe—his faith.

"You cheated me!" the being roared, the ferocity in its voice shaking the fragile walls of nearby buildings.

Landry countered. "It was you who cheated *me*. You knew the cards in my hand, and you knew I couldn't win. But then again, I did."

A slimy tongue accompanied by a nauseating stench flicked out as the demon wheezed, "Tell me, you cheating little scumbag. Where did you get the ace of spades?"

"It was a parting gift from Jack Blair. Now bring him back to life and get out of Midnight Pass."

The creature hovered above Landry, flapping its scaly red wings as it hissed, "This isn't over. Be on your guard always, my clever friend. My battle with you is far from finished." It raised its mighty head upward, rose into the clouds, and disappeared.

Landry stood alone in the street, wondering when the next chapter would begin.

CHAPTER FORTY-ONE

Cate kept her thoughts to herself as Landry attempted to describe the fantastic situation that defied description. It was a superhero action movie, a Grimm's fairy tale and a fearsome horror novel all rolled into one brief face-off that ended with the antagonist tossing threats and exiting the scene.

She asked a trick question. "What time is your flight home?" She knew he hadn't scheduled one, because he wasn't finished there. This was his modus operandi, but she wanted to hear his answer before she opened the floodgates.

"Just a few loose ends to tie up," he said. He understood her concerns, but he had to stay until the authorities were finished with him. Finding the bodies in the cabinet was no ordinary discovery—these people had vanished over decades, and only he could explain much of what was happening in Midnight Pass. His answers would necessarily involve the supernatural because everything in this cursed town lay outside the boundaries of reason and logic. And those answers would be unacceptable to the lawmen, but that was of no concern because Landry knew the truth.

His primary reason for staying longer was to find Jack. After the card game, he'd gone straight back to the cabinet, and to his relief, Jack's body wasn't with the others. Lucifer had promised if Landry won, he'd give Jack's life back, but under the circumstances, he wondered if it would happen. Meanwhile, he would have to keep looking.

Cate listened to all his logic, but she wouldn't have it this time. "No, Landry. You have to get away from there today. That thing—the devil, I guess—threatened you. Please. I beg you to run. If Jack comes back, then that's wonderful. But he's missing, and you still have a chance. Come home now. I don't want to lose you too."

"Soon. As soon as I can, Cate. I promise." She disconnected, frustrated, scared and wishing she could force him back.

He called Chief Hawkins to come down, and while he waited, Landry tackled his next task, gathering information off the reading glasses he had worn during the card game. With 20/20 eyesight, he needed no corrective lenses, but these were no ordinary glasses. They came straight out of Henri's arsenal of paranormal investigative equipment, and Landry had brought them along, thinking they might come in handy. Now he had his fingers crossed that they had.

Built into the frame were a tiny camera, microphone and micro SD memory card. Landry had turned on the apparatus when he entered the saloon, and if everything had worked correctly, he'd have captured the card game and his opponent's fury, although in Midnight Pass one could never be certain if equipment would work or not. If he'd been successful, he would have unique footage of a creature—the devil, for God's sake—as he morphed from human to a loathsome creature. This video would tell it all, because Landry hadn't the words to sufficiently describe the magnitude of what had happened.

He sat in the old pickup, plugged the memory card into an adapter connected to his laptop, and waited. Following a moment of grainy snow, a picture flashed on the screen. This was what he'd hoped for. He whooped aloud as the scene unfolded: the rowdy saloon, the hostess who took him to the back room, and his conversations with Luce were all there. So was the card game and—most important of all—Luce's thunderous, terrifying reaction to Landry's winning hand and his sudden departure into the skies.

This was priceless. Despite some quality issues that could be overcome, this stunning footage would provide the amazing climax to the next episode in his *Mysterious America* television series. This one would be a first—the tragic tale of the devil, what he did in a little Florida town, and a card game played for human lives. One thought permeated his very soul—if only Jack were safe.

He saved the video to his hard drive and emailed it to Phil Vandegriff, asking him not to mention it until Landry's return. Cate had heard his description of what had happened. but if she saw the video, she would be in Florida tomorrow, dragging him home.

———

After Landry showed Chief Hawkins the horror cabinet, the lawman sent photos to Sheriff Warner in Key West and then called to say he couldn't ignore the ghost town any longer. Warner agreed and asked the chief to lead the investigation with him, a gesture Hawkins appreciated and one Landry thought made a great deal of sense, given the chief's involvement from the beginning. That same day the sheriff, three deputies and two men from the county medical examiner's office drove up from Key West to assess the situation and take possession of the corpses in the vault.

In the tightly knit community of Everglades City, everyone was aware the famous paranormal investigator Landry Drake had been staying at the Ivey House. Although people speculated about why he'd come, almost no one knew for sure, but when a small convoy from Key West—two sheriff's cruisers, a medical examiner's sedan and a box truck, also from the ME's office—drove through town that morning, heading south, rumors flew like leaves in a summer squall. All those law enforcement people were on a dead-end road that led to only one place.

To deter the press and the curious, Warner stationed Deputy McCarty at the barricade and two others at the gates leading into Midnight Pass. The first media outlet on the scene was a satellite truck from the ABC affiliate in Naples. When they were told they could go no further, the reporter and cameraman set up shop in situ. After unsuccessfully badgering Deputy McCarty for information, they aired a brief "breaking news" story live from what everyone was beginning to believe was the scene of a mass murder.

Anyone with a police band radio—and there were plenty in the Everglades—knew that a number of bodies had been discovered in an old bank vault in Midnight Pass. Nobody knew the details—who the deceased were, how their bodies were displayed, how long they'd been there, and who found them, for instance—because Sheriff Warner didn't know those things himself until he got to the site. Once he saw the chamber of horrors, he kept a tight lid on things. He considered Midnight Pass to be a freak show that got more bizarre with every revelation, and having what he told his men was "a damned ghost hunter" around didn't help the situation.

Those who'd worked with Landry—his deputy Tim McCarty and Chief Hawkins—believed in the guy and swore he was on the up and up, but Warner still couldn't accept what he called supernatural mumbo-jumbo. Regardless, he couldn't bar Landry from staying in Midnight Pass, because most of what had occurred was because of him.

Unlike those who had perished in the hurricane, the bodies hanging in the cabinet were crime victims—unfortunates who had found themselves in Midnight Pass accidentally or on purpose, encountered what Sheriff Warner believed to be a serial killer, and met their fates.

Landry knew better, of course. The serial killer wasn't a human; he was Lucifer himself. And it was about time the victims got some attention. Those thirteen people who disappeared between 1935 and the present had been ignored both by the media and law enforcement, and Landry couldn't understand why nobody cared enough to search for a common thread. Frustrated families had surely badgered the authorities, and the sheriffs who served Monroe County over the decades probably weren't incompetent or callous. They simply didn't have the resources to investigate one-off disappearances every decade or so in a faraway ghost town.

Over two days the authorities gathered evidence and duly recorded Landry's increasingly bizarre revelations and videos exposing the truth about Midnight Pass. At the end, they loaded the bodies for transport to the medical examiner's office in Key West, and when it was time to abandon the premises, Sheriff Warner took Landry aside.

"I don't like the way you operate, Drake," he said. "You may have swept the people of Everglades City off their feet and got them all pumped up thinking they're going to be on TV, but you've ruined a crime scene, and I ought to charge you with destroying evidence. You and Chief Hawkins should have called me before you ever went to Midnight Pass—"

Landry interrupted. "We tried, Sheriff. Chief Hawkins called, and you sent Deputy McCarty for a couple of days, but you wouldn't let him stay. You weren't interested in Midnight Pass, and you told the chief to handle it himself. Until I found the bodies, nobody cared one bit if I came here or not. Now that it's a problem for you, you want to wish it away. Sorry, but it's too late. Speaking of your being interested, what are you going to do about my friend Jack Blair? He's still missing."

Warner said, "Is he? I'm not sure I believe you. After you showed me that cockamamie horror-flick home movie you concocted, where you're playing cards with the devil, I don't think there's much you can tell me that I'll believe. You're in this for the publicity, and I'm not real big on sensationalism. Folks down here like things quiet, and all you've done is stir them up. I think it's best if you forget about putting anything on television about Midnight Pass."

"Are you serious? You think I'd ignore this place? Things happened here that are completely beyond belief. And you're suggesting I just forget it?"

He moved a step closer and stuck his finger in Landry's chest. "You're a smart guy. And it's more than a suggestion."

With a grim smile, Landry shook his head. "No way. You and everybody else ignored the disappearances for years. It took my friend vanishing and my coming down here to get anybody interested. What happened is sad and grisly and depressing, but it's unearthly too, and I was right in the middle of it. I experienced things here I can't explain—supernatural things—and I promise you this. Absolutely without a doubt there's going to be a show about this place."

"There'd better not be a word about me or my department, and I don't want you contacting any of my men either. I'll haul your ass in so fast…"

It was too late for grandstanding. "Don't worry, Sheriff," he said. "I'll make sure every word we use is the truth and nothing but. And I'll interview anybody who has something to add. After all, even down here where people like things quiet, it's still a free country, right?"

On that sour note, everyone piled into their vehicles and drove away, leaving Midnight Pass abandoned once again and Jack Blair still on the unaccounted list.

CHAPTER FORTY-TWO

Jack's homecoming was as inexplicable as his disappearance from the cabinet of horrors had been. It happened on a bright morning just two days after Landry returned to New Orleans. He stood staring absently out the conference room window when he noticed someone sitting in the recessed entryway of the building across the street. Thinking it was a vagrant taking a break from panhandling on Bourbon Street, he turned away, then looked back as he realized the person looked familiar.

Landry bounded down the stairs two at a time, raced through the passageway that led from the courtyard to the front door, and darted across Toulouse Street, oblivious to traffic. He dodged a beer truck, its horn blaring and brakes squealing, and ran straight to where the man sat.

"Jack! Jack, you've come home!"

The man bowed his head and said nothing, leading Landry to think he'd made a mistake. But then Jack looked up and muttered, "Home. It might have been better if I hadn't come."

"Are you all right? Can you walk?" He offered him

an arm, which Jack looked at blankly before taking hold and allowing Landry to hoist him up. "Come on. Let's get you upstairs. Are you hungry? Thirsty? Where have you been?"

"Later. Talk later," he mumbled as he took a moment to steady himself before clinging tightly to Landry's arm and stumbling across the street. The stairwell was too narrow for them to walk side by side, and Landry tripped more than once while clumsily trying to guide Jack up.

Cate and Henri rushed over, hesitating as they saw the confusion in his face. "Something's not right. Let's give him a little time," Landry said, steering him to the couch, where he collapsed and sat staring off into the room. Landry stayed with him while Cate left a voicemail for his girlfriend, Caryn, who was at work, and spoke to Ted Carpenter, his boss at Channel Nine. The station was three blocks away, and Ted, certainly no fan of exercise, arrived in record time. Huffing and puffing up the stairs, he burst into the room and ran to Jack's side.

"Hey, buddy! Gosh, I'm glad to see you. We've missed you at the station…"

Jack slowly raised his head and looked into Ted's face. "I want…I want…"

"What do you want? Just say the word."

"I want it to end, but it isn't over. Not for me or for Landry or for the next one he captures. It isn't over. How will it end?" Ted had no idea what he was talking about, and Landry let it go, having no desire to begin an hour-long summary of the latest events in south Florida.

Late that afternoon when Caryn White arrived, Jack greeted her with the same blank expression and didn't respond to her hugs. She cried a little and agreed with Cate that Jack should stay with them for a while. Landry had been in Midnight Pass, and if Jack snapped out of whatever this was, it would be best if he were nearby.

For a couple of days their attempts to revive his spirits met with no success. They all tried to help him, but everyone led busy lives, and none had the skills or the time to bring Jack back out of his bad place. Caryn suggested he see a professional, but Jack refused to go.

Although he took in his surroundings and replied when spoken to, he seemed depressed and disconnected from the present. He sat where Landry told him to sit and watched them work, but on the rare occasion when he initiated a conversation, he'd often stop mid-sentence as if trying to capture a lost thought. Any discussion about his life and his career in television prior to going to Midnight Pass confused him.

His breakthrough came during the third night. Landry wasn't sleeping much, and he got up when he heard the kitchen cabinet doors open and close. He found Jack there, holding a glass and looking for a Dr Pepper. Just by his voice Landry could tell his friend was back. He asked if they could talk, Jack agreed, and they sat at the dining table.

"Can you tell me what happened?"

"Not a lot happened to me. I told you earlier I was in my old house on Knight Street in Memphis most of the time. You saw me there as a kid, playing ball in the front yard. The boy wasn't me, of course. He was an illusion, but I watched you from my window. I tried to call out, but I couldn't. Luce kept me confined there, and he had some kind of lock on my senses."

"But you texted me for help. You asked me to find you."

"Not me. Luce did that. He was taunting you."

"But how about when I saw you in the vault? You handed me a deck of cards, and I used it to play the game with Lucifer. Was that an illusion too?"

"No. That was the only time I came to you. I tried to convince you it was actually me, but you became angry because I couldn't do more. Luce sent me there to give you advice about how to play the game with him and to hand you that deck of cards. He hadn't had a challenge in eons, and he gave you the illusion of advantage to make his own win even more satisfying. He's a deceiver, Landry. You should have known he'd never play fair."

"Play fair? You were my friend, but you gave me a rigged deck of cards, and then he killed you. I saw your body hanging in the cabinet, and you had the ace of spades in your pocket. You gave me the card that let me win."

"You're on the wrong track about everything. Every body hanging in that cabinet was real but mine. It was just another illusion. And about that playing card—I didn't give it to you. I couldn't have; Luce would never have allowed it because it flipped the odds in your favor."

"So who…"

"You've overlooked this more than once, Landry. The answer's simple; think about someone in the background watching over you time and again. Think about an old man wearing a baseball cap."

CHAPTER FORTY-THREE

At last it seemed the ordeal in Midnight Pass was over. Nothing had happened for weeks, and sometimes Landry went for days without having flashbacks or dreams. Things were busy around the studio as the crew worked on the episode. The footage from the drone and everything Phil, Henri and Landry had recorded required extensive editing. Voiceovers, background material, and still shots of the cremation pyre and a town filled with blackened buildings had to be added to the mix, and Landry worked on a sidebar about the bank vault's Depression-era records, coins and currency.

Jack had returned to Channel Nine, easing himself back into the routine of investigative reporting and seemingly improving every day. Locked away in a fantasy world in his own childhood bedroom, he had missed much of the horror that had played out in Midnight Pass, although he knew his captor's identity, and the reality that he could face torture and a hideous death at any time had scarred his mind with wounds that only the passage of time could heal.

Landry and Phil were in the third-floor cutting

room, editing video, when the call came. Landry recognized the 239 south Florida area code, but not the number. He answered, listened for a moment, said he'd call back and disconnected. He summoned the others to the conference room, opened an email on his laptop, and clicked on the attachment it contained.

"Chief Hawkins just sent over a video. Says it's urgent. I'm supposed to call him back, and then we watch it together." He placed the call.

The chief led off with an apology. "After what all of us experienced down here, this is a hard call to make. We were duped, all of us. You all left Midnight Pass thinking the horrors were over, but now it's happened again. A girl disappeared down there yesterday, and it was captured on the video I sent you. Start it up, and let's take a look."

They watched Marnie Vogt, a fourteen-year-old resident of Everglades City, explain that she was about to ride her bicycle to Midnight Pass. Intrigued about the bodies that had been found, Marnie had decided to make a cool movie for TikTok about the mysteries of the spooky old ghost town.

Live-streaming as she walked the empty streets, Marnie visited the cremation pyre and returned to the bank, where she made her way into the lobby and began a commentary about the bodies that had been found behind the round steel door before her.

The chief said, "Look closely now. See the tendrils of wispy smoke start coming out from behind the door? From here it gets bizarre. She's unaware the tendril things are circling around her, moving up from her feet until it looks like she's halfway in a cocoon. Watch now, right here when she realizes something's wrong, starts screaming, and drops her phone to the floor. It's aimed up and records gray sky through the destroyed roof beams."

Just then the background noise stopped as if the audio had been turned off. Chief Hawkins was silent too, for so long that Landry thought he'd lost the connection.

"Chief, are you there?"

"Yeah, I'm here. That audio issue is part of it somehow. Keep watching."

Now another person was present, someone who picked up the phone and aimed it down at the girl lying unconscious amid the rubble on the floor. He kept the camera on her and took hold of her leg, her torso making scraping, scratching noises as he dragged her toward the vault. When Landry realized what was coming—that she was about to become the next victim in the cabinet, he shouted, "No! No, dammit! Let her go!"

The video portion went blank, but the audio continued with a giggle—a laugh that began low and throaty, increasing in intensity and volume until it was a high-pitched, drawn-out cackle. Then came the words.

"You thought you won, but you didn't. Can't cheat the devil. Gotcha, Landry Drake!"

That was the end.

Everyone sat in shock for a moment; Cate spoke first. "I...I can't believe this. You beat Lucifer. He left Midnight Pass. How can this happen again?"

A voice came from behind them. "Lucifer told you it wasn't over. He said your battle was far from finished. He's inviting you back for the second round."

Startled, they whirled around. *What the hell is Jack doing here?*

He had more to say. "He won't stop until you're dead, Landry. You're the only one who can end this."

———

Late that afternoon, after a frantic rush to catch a plane and a hundred-mile-an-hour drive south from Fort Myers in a siren-shrieking convoy of lit-up sheriff's cruisers, Landry, Cate and Henri waited anxiously as Chief Hawkins and Deputy McCarty tugged open the massive vault door. Phil's camera caught everything as they rushed inside, passed through the narrow opening into the cash vault, and threw open the double cabinet doors. The row of hooks was still there, a grim reminder of thirteen bodies that had hung there only days earlier.

But this time they thanked God they found the cabinet empty. Still missing, Marnie Vogt certainly wasn't safe, but whatever Luce had done with her, at least she hadn't been sacrificed and mounted like yet another trophy in his case.

Jack couldn't explain how he knew to come to their office when the TikTok video played. It had been a feeling—something urging him to go. Once he said his piece, everyone knew why he came. He served as messenger, reminding Landry that the battle was yet to be decided. The girl was a pawn to get him back to Midnight Pass, and Landry had accepted the bait. He was here, and it was time to settle this affair for good.

CHAPTER FORTY-FOUR

Adjacent to a stone crab processing plant five minutes' walk from the Ivey House stood a sheet-iron building that housed the Tipsy Tuna. After noticing it the other day, he'd chosen the dingy bar this afternoon because its atmosphere matched Landry's pensive mood. Country music blared, pool balls clicked, and the ceiling fans were no match for the cigar and cigarette smoke that hung overhead like a Midnight Pass storm cloud. Ignored by the other patrons, he sat at the bar and stared into the double vodka tonic in front of him.

He'd left Cate at the inn, explaining that he needed time to think, to get his mind around the fact that both Jack's abduction and the teenaged girl's were his fault. Luce Moros—the man who wasn't a man—wanted Landry's soul, and as long as Landry continued to resist, innocent people's lives were at stake. The card game should have ended it all, but Luce lied, and Landry cheated, so it ended in a draw with nothing settled. The devil, in the form of a prehistoric flying reptile, had left him standing in the street with a warning that the battle was far from over.

He rarely lied to Cate, and then only when he thought a lie would protect her, but he'd done so today. It was true he needed time to think, but he had already received his answer. All that remained was how to make it happen, and the answer had come to Landry late last night, not as a gauzy, translucent dream but as a revelation, an epiphany, a moment of reckoning that exploded into his thoughts like a fireworks celebration on the Fourth of July. It was not a good thing—certainly not the solution he'd have chosen—but he'd asked for an answer, and he would live with it.

When they'd crawled into bed last evening, he confided his fears to Cate. The cause was lost. There was nothing more he could do because Lucifer couldn't be beaten. He'd wanted Landry back, and that was the price Landry must pay. He could only hope the missing girl Marnie Vogt was still alive, and that Lucifer would swap her for Landry.

"No!" she'd cried over and over, pounding her fists on his chest. "I won't let you do it. Your going there won't help anything. He may not let the girl go, and if he does, then you've traded your life for hers. It makes no sense."

That was when he told the big lie, promising he wouldn't do anything rash despite knowing that was exactly what he was planning. After that draining conversation, he had fallen into an agonizing, churning chasm between sleeping and waking, but at 2:38 a.m. his eyes shot open, and he sat bolt upright in bed. He had his answer. He knew how to erase Midnight Pass and all its woes from the landscape, never to have it lure an unsuspecting stranger into its ghostly streets and its cabinet of horror again.

Tomorrow he would go to Midnight Pass alone, face the enemy, and surrender if that was what it took. This awful, final solution swept over him while somehow giving him peace. It was the proper thing to do…and the only way to stop Lucifer from continuing the madness. Landry was the person he wanted, and so it would be.

"Another?" the bartender asked, pointing to his empty glass. Landry nodded and frowned as a man took the adjacent barstool. Why here? There were plenty of other places. He hoped to hell this guy didn't want to strike up a conversation about the paranormal. He cupped his new drink and glanced over when the man removed his hat and placed it on the bar. An Astros ball cap.

Landry raised his head and looked at the same blue flannel shirt, bib overalls and tall work boots. Decades older than Landry, the old man next to him sported a head of white hair and a day-old stubble of beard.

"I guess I should thank you for giving me the ace of spades…twice. Who are you?"

"It's all about the memories. Haven't you figured that out by now? That's his stock in trade—memories. Everything in Midnight Pass is tied to memories of things that used to be. Luce finds a memory in your subconscious and creates a scene complete with backdrops and characters. You take it from there, embellishing and adding parts until it's whole. By then you've bought in, and he's got you where he wants you."

Landry sniffed. "Whatever. None of that matters anymore. I know what I'm going to do. What's your role in all this? Are you another one of his creations?"

The old man gave a hearty laugh. "Hardly. You're going at this the wrong way. You think you got your answer last night in a dream, but if you do what you're planning, he wins, and nothing changes."

"But it will change because this is all about me."

Another chuckle. "All about you. Now we're getting a bit smug. If it were only that simple. He's a liar, a deceiver. You know that. Jack told you, but you already knew it. What makes you think he'll stop if you give in to him?"

"I don't know. I don't know anything, to tell the truth. But in the here and now, I believe I'm the only one who can make him stop. But what about you? Are you who I think you are?"

He shrugged. "That depends. If you believe giving up will solve things, then you haven't figured anything out. You'd be a fool to face him without a plan. No human has done it, although many have tried."

"Will you face him with me?"

"No, I'm not in the game. I'm your coach."

Landry's phone vibrated. He pulled it from his back pocket, silenced it, and said, "Sorry about that," but the barstool next to his was empty. The bartender was five feet away; Landry waved him over and said, "Where did the guy next to me go?"

"Next to you? Buddy, that seat's been empty ever since you walked in here. Is everything okay?"

Landry smiled. "Yeah, everything's good. It's time for me to tab out. I have stuff to do."

CHAPTER FORTY-FIVE

To be able to summon an Uber driver in a tiny town like Everglades City surprised Landry. Without a vehicle and unwilling to bring anyone else into the situation, he'd have been hitchhiking otherwise. The driver, a friendly girl in a ten-year-old Chrysler, was surprised when Landry went by a bookstore and then asked to be dropped at the barricade. He'd evaded her small talk until she quit trying, given her a cash tip at the end, and waited until she was out of sight before he started the three-mile walk to town. In his mind he ran through the new plan he'd devised. It had come into his brain like a flash the moment the old man left the bar. He had no idea what would happen, but at least he'd start out playing offense.

Under crystal blue skies he approached the gate and passed through. He ignored the dark clouds and droplets of rain that suddenly appeared. They were merely backdrops for the stage play that would be performed soon. The town was quiet and empty, and Landry felt a sense of nostalgia as he walked past now-familiar places. The Security State Bank, which held the ghastly cabinet of horrors; the town square, where a band had played in the gazebo on Labor Day; the pile of lumber that had provided the fiery end to a hundred and sixty-two shrouded bodies; and his own house on his street in Jeanerette.

Everything in Midnight Pass was real in the sense that things conjured in one's mind can seem real. He had seen things, touched things, experienced and felt and hurt, and all of those things had been real.

Why did this have to happen to me? I had a good thing going, a wonderful life with Cate and my friends and work. I love investigating the paranormal, but look where that's gotten me. I saved Jack—at least I think he's safe—but I've lost my own life. I'm thirty-two years old, standing here in a haunted town, waiting for God knows what, yet ready for whatever comes next. Was I too cocky? Did I take too many risks and ignore everybody's warnings? Am I a fool after all? All I want to know is why it had to happen to me.

Someone called out, "I'm here for you." It was Cate's familiar voice; he spun around to see her coming down the middle of the street with Henri and Phil behind her. Jack was there too; they waved and called out, "We're all rooting for you, Landry."

This can't be happening. I left everyone back at the Ivey House when I went to that bar.

They gathered around him and wrapped him in bear hugs until he pulled away and shouted, "You're not here! This isn't real. He's doing this to me—creating an image for me to cling to and believe in—and you aren't real!"

A huge poof of smoke worthy of a Vegas magic show enveloped the four, and when it dissipated seconds later, Luce Moros stood where they had been. "Do you realize how much more perceptive you are now than when all this began?" he asked. "You've become quite the skeptic. I thought you believed in the paranormal."

"Let the girl go. I'm here to finish this, and I want

you to promise me you'll release Jack's soul, free her, and leave Midnight Pass as you promised."

"My, what a martyr, yet what you ask this time is reasonable. You cheated me, and no one cheats me. You now understand the error of your ways, and I agree to your feeble demands. I promise to release the girl and your friend's soul. Once you and I are finished here, I will leave Midnight Pass. There are plenty of other places that deserve my attention, I promise you. Someday soon people may hear about a catastrophic event accompanied by wailing and sobbing as hundreds die. When they hear of unspeakable horror, they should think of me, Landry Drake. Now, shall we conclude this?"

As Luce took a step toward Landry, he removed a small New Testament from his back pocket and held it high. "Back off, Satan! You can't conquer me! I can repel anything you throw at me, because I have the power of God with me!"

"Miserable, despicable creature! Do you think a book of words can stop me? Do you know how many humans have vainly attempted to end my control over their lives with that book?" With a mighty roar, he split his body as he had done before. This time he emerged as a ten-foot-long iguana-like reptile with four fat legs, its forked tongue flicking here and there as its beady eyes surveyed Landry. When it took a step forward, Landry feinted, accidentally dropping the Bible to the ground. The reptile raced over, snatched it up with a claw, and ripped it to shreds.

Landry prepared to stand his ground and fight to the end, but the creature mutated into something larger and more fearsome than before—a birdlike thing twenty feet tall, its head at the end of a long neck that twisted about in the air. As its powerful beak arced toward Landry and it stretched its scaly wings to a span of more than thirty feet, he jumped backward, tripped and landed flat on his back. A twelve-inch talon struck Landry's chest, pinning him down.

"One little push and it's all over for you," the thing hissed. "Your life is worth nothing, and I should release you from your miserable existence now. But you're going to suffer, you pitiful wretch!" As the pressure increased and he gasped for breath, flashes of white light shot through Landry's brain. He felt consciousness slipping away, and his head lolled to one side. A hazy memory that might have been real floated into his mind as he noticed something close by.

Thigh-high work boots, grimy and mud-caked.

Rivulets of blood ran down his chest as the beast's razor-sharp nail pierced his skin.

He struggled, barely conscious now. With a mighty effort, he twisted his head and looked around. Everything came to him in hazy swirls of gray, and only one thing became clear—a figure wearing an Astros ball cap.

The force of the creature's claw began to push the remaining air from Landry's lungs.

He thought, *Lord, save me from this creature.*

Aloud. Words formed in his brain, or perhaps someone was saying them. *Aloud. You have to pray aloud.*

With a tremendous heave, he sucked in a last gulp of precious air and screamed, "Lord, save…save me from this creature…"

Instantly the being lifted its claw and receded. Lying on his back, gasping for air, Landry saw movement to his right. The man from the bar—the old fellow wearing the flannel shirt—stood with his right arm raised high into the air. In it he held an ordinary garden rake pointed toward the serpent. Gale-force winds arose, sweeping over the town, threatening the fragile structures, and screeching like a banshee.

The deafening winds howled until the moment the man spoke. From the mouth of this peasant farmer flowed forceful, commanding words in a voice that resounded like the crashing, thundering crescendo of an orchestra. They rolled across the skies, a thousand times more powerful than the winds, demonstrating his raw power.

"Stand up, Landry! This is *your* battle! Stand up for yourself!"

That amazing voice should have instilled confidence, but Landry felt defeat. Words couldn't stop a being like the one he faced. The old man…or whatever he was…seemed confident enough, but could anyone beat the devil?

With a mighty effort, Landry struggled to obey the man, gasping for breath as he clumsily rose to his feet. The old man approached him, stuck something in his shirt pocket, patted it, and said, "You have the power to defeat him. Trust in yourself, trust in me, and finish this."

With that bit of encouragement, Landry bucked up and implemented his new plan. As the mighty creature bent and swayed in the air above him, Landry focused his mind on a scene from a night long, long ago—a memory of home and family and the best night ever.

CHAPTER FORTY-SIX

It was the most wonderful Christmas I would ever experience. I was seven, and we were still a real family because Dad was still alive. Maybe he knew it was his last one, because he went all out, doing stuff we never did before or after. He hung lights from the eaves of our house, took us to the woods outside of town to choose and cut our own tree, and stood in line with us at the mall so we could tell Santa exactly what we wanted.

On Christmas Eve we had turkey and dressing and sweet potatoes and everything else that made that dinner special, and it was the best meal I ever ate. After dinner, as was our tradition, we left the table and went straight to the living room for family gift exchange. Santa would come down the chimney tonight, but on Christmas Eve we got to open presents from Mom and Dad.

First things first. We sat on the floor around Dad's chair while he got the tattered old Bible, turned to Luke, and read the Christmas story. There was something magical about it this time, because it would never happen in our little family again. As he finished and closed the

Bible, the doorbell rang. My brother, Larry, and I rushed to see who it was and found a group of Salvation Army carolers in the yard. They sang one of our favorites, "God Rest Ye Merry Gentlemen," and their voices sounded like a Heavenly choir. Those lyrics—those special words meant so much.

Sweating and panting like a marathon runner, Landry was exhausted after having exerted all the energy he could muster to concentrate on the best Christmas of his life. He had emphasized every detail—every recollection of what made that time special, and now he paused to look at the beast, who was watching him closely but not moving against him. It was as if the creature didn't know what to make of Landry's performance.

The next stage of Landry's plan was to sing that favorite carol aloud. He was no entertainer, but today he sang like Pavarotti, taking things as slowly as he dared and belting out the key words he wanted the beast to hear.

"Let nothing you dismay, Remember Christ...was born...to save us all from Satan's power..."

When he stopped, the stillness was absolute—no wind, no rain, nothing broke the silence. Landry stood facing the reptile, twenty feet from it, and the old man waited in the shadow of a nearby building. Mustering what strength remained, Landry screamed, "You have no place here!" With his words, the beast began to undulate, rising into the air to attack, and the old man stepped out of the shadows, taking his place beside Landry and tossing the garden rake to him.

The man cried out, "Now do it! Raise your stick and order the demon out!"

Landry looked at the rake blankly for a second, this wasn't part of any plan, and he wasn't certain what to do. Wouldn't the old man be better to deal with ousting demons? The monster reared back and flicked its tongue as words flowed into Landry's mind. Not words he created, but words that formed and flowed to his lips like water.

Looking every bit like Moses parting the Red Sea, Landry raised the rake in his outstretched arm, shook it and screamed, "Lucifer, rebellious creature that you are, I banish you from this place forever! Leave the girl. Leave Jack. Leave this town. Go to hell, Satan! Go to hell!"

For the first time since September 1935, the clouds disappeared over Midnight Pass, and bright sunshine bathed the streets in a warm glow. The balmy rays had a remarkable effect on the serpentine creature, which drew back in revulsion, howled and scratched as if its scaly skin were on fire, frantically searched for a dark place to shelter, and with one earth-shattering shriek underwent a massive transformation. Within seconds the thing was gone; now Landry faced Luce Moros—Lucifer in human form.

"What do I do now?" Landry cried, but the old man no longer stood beside him. He panicked, and the ever-observant Luce cackled in delight.

"You *leave*, Landry. That's what you do now. I stay here, and you leave. You put on quite a show, but you lost."

Losing his nerve, Landry hesitated a moment. "*You* will leave! And you will do everything you promised!" He stumbled on the words as terror flooded his brain. He didn't have the courage to keep going.

Then he remembered the old man's words. *Trust in me, trust in yourself, and finish this!*

He smiled grimly. He had beaten this opponent once. All he had to do was repeat the process.

Hoisting the rake into the air once more, he screamed, "I pray for the girl Marnie Vogt. I pray for Jack Blair's soul. I pray for peace in Midnight Pass. I trust in God to make Lucifer keep his promises and banish him to hell. Leave this place. Your reign here is over, Satan!"

An enormous bolt of lightning streaked out of the cloudless sky, striking Luce in the chest. His body burst into white-hot flames, and with a shriek that resounded into the heavens, he disintegrated into a pile of ashes.

Landry raised his hands into the air. “It’s over,” he shouted to the one hundred and sixty-two people who died in Midnight Pass. “He’s gone!” he screamed to the ones who disappeared after the hurricane. No one answered, of course, because he was completely alone.

As he turned to go, he heard something else in his mind.

It happened because you trusted.

CHAPTER FORTY-SEVEN

All he wanted now was to take a victory lap, to make one last stroll down the sunlit streets before leaving Midnight Pass forever. As he walked, his phone vibrated. It was Cate.

"I'm sorry I left you…"

She cried, "Oh my God, Landry. Are you all right?"

"It's…uh, it's over. I won. I beat him, Cate. Not me, actually, but with some help…"

"Stop, Landry. I saw it all! I watched it happen. I saw you raise that stick against that raging monster! I saw you face him down, and I saw Luce blown to smithereens!"

"How could you see it? What are you talking about?"

"It happened in my mind. A few minutes ago—just as it was happening to you, I guess—a bright flash of light blinded me. I hoped I wasn't having a heart attack. I closed my eyes and watched the scene play out. You were there, and so was the old man and that creature. That man gave you advice and handed you the rake, and you took it from there. You even sang Christmas carols…"

"Part of a plan, actually. I don't know if that part did any good or not."

"I saw that old farmer put something in your shirt pocket. What was it?"

Landry had forgotten all about that incident, and he reached in and removed a playing card. The ace of spades. "I guess this worked for me twice," he commented, turning it between his fingers.

"You did it!" she cried. "I've never seen anything like it."

"Because of him. He told me he'd be my coach. He gave me courage and strength and made the devil keep his promises. But, Cate, who…who was he? Could he have been…"

"You know the answer. Somewhere in your mind or in your heart, you know."

And at that moment in Midnight Pass, Florida, the town was filled with the music of high-pitched tinkling bells—the sounds of a bell choir at a Christmas Eve service, Landry thought with a smile.

He fell to his knees. *Thank you for everything.*

———

Advance publicity for the upcoming documentary about Midnight Pass was in high gear. In the weeks after Landry's final showdown, Phil Vandegriff and a crew from the Paranormal Network spent more time there, filming the end not only of the episode, but the final days of the town itself.

Landry lent his name to a grassroots effort that aimed to spare Midnight Pass from further mayhem. For over eighty years no one had returned to claim loved ones or property or anything else. The hurricane had taken its toll, and the survivors shunned the place as though the inhabitants were at fault. Given that lack of concern, a group of interested citizens in Collier County formed a committee to right the wrongs. When Emma Tate, the docent at the Everglades City museum who'd helped Landry during his visits, asked Landry to be honorary chairman, he accepted without hesitation.

Despite his busy schedule, Landry made another trip to Florida, this time to Tallahassee, where he met with representatives of the Florida emergency management office. There were millions in state and federal funds earmarked for disaster relief, and he convinced the governor and legislative leaders to spend some of it in Midnight Pass. He also championed a bill that gave the Museum of the Everglades rights to any property in the town deemed historically significant.

After the walls of the bank building were razed and it was safe to enter, museum employees and patrons spent hours in the vault, completing a comprehensive inventory. Safety-deposit boxes were drilled and contents reunited with heirs where possible. Bank records from the 1930s provided a fascinating look into everyday life during the Depression.

Once everything salvageable had been retrieved, the disaster relief money was used to take the town down to the ground. The cremation pyre was buried, and every ruined structure in town was bulldozed. Grass and trees were planted, and soon the area bore no resemblance to the place of sadness and horror it had been.

Over the coming months, the museum would sell most of the bank's coins and currency for far more than face value, raising enough to build an annex to house the Midnight Pass exhibit. In that area, visitors could view photographs, see some of Landry's videos, and marvel at an amazing array of memorabilia from stores and businesses, including a 1935 Ford convertible straight off the showroom floor.

A special room housed an exhibit about the paranormal and the unexplained. On display were the rake

Landry shook at the demon, the glasses Landry used to record the card game with Luce Moros, video clips showing the town's mysteries, and the tragic journal penned by Nancy Stallings, head cashier of Security State Bank of Midnight Pass, as they waited to die in the vault. Thanks to public service announcements that ran on local stations and Landry's network, tourism swelled in the area, and Everglades City profited from the sadness.

Chief Hawkins had a cameo role in Landry's production, as did fourteen-year-old Marnie Vogt, the last person to disappear in Midnight Pass. During her two days as a captive, Luce had kept her in a state of limbo, apparently awaiting Landry's return for the rematch. After collapsing in a dead faint in front of the vault door during her TikTok video, she awoke in her bed at home in Midnight Pass with no recollection of time passing or anything that had happened to her. After watching her own video, Marnie would become a lifelong fan of Landry's because she had been a part of the paranormal herself.

Landry, Cate, Henri and Jack sat in his favorite corner table at Muriel's just off Jackson Square in the French Quarter. They reminisced about the struggles each had experienced in Midnight Pass, and how their modern-day woes were nothing compared to the work done by the thing who called himself Luce Moros. He'd started it all, bringing the hurricane in for a direct hit just to stir things up, in his own words. He'd kept things going for decades, kidnapping unsuspecting people to keep his personal game going.

If Henri hadn't picked up the story and insisted Landry and Cate go from Siesta Key to investigate, it might all still be going on today, but now things would be better for everyone, the living and the dead.

Jack's experience had been an ordeal for everyone.

He'd suffered mentally and physically, but today he was back in top form and apparently none the worse for what he'd been through. "I never gave much thought to religious stuff like souls," he admitted, "but once you risked everything for mine not once but twice, I decided I'd better change my thinking. Do you really think we have our souls back now? I realize there's no way to be sure, so how do you know?"

Landry agreed it was impossible to know, but he said the peace and contentment that came with knowing a higher being existed was sufficient for him. They talked about the old man who dressed in work clothes and dirty boots. "If he was who we think," Landry said, "why would he appear like that? I expected flowing robes and a crown or a halo or angels flying all around. He looked like a commoner."

"Just like us," Cate whispered. "Isn't it wonderful that he looked just like us?"

"There was one thing I never understood," Landry said. "The old man always wore an Astros baseball cap. You think that's a coincidence, don't you? You don't think he…in his position and all that…do you think he's actually an Astros fan?"

"Maybe so." Cate laughed. "After all, they won the World Series."

Thank you for reading *Midnight Pass.*

If you enjoyed it, I'd appreciate a review on Amazon. Reviews are what allow other readers to find books they enjoy, so thanks in advance for your help.

Please join me on:

Facebook

http://on.fb.me/187NRRP

Twitter

@BThompsonBooks

This is book 2 of the Mysterious America series. The others are available as paperbacks or ebooks.

MAY WE OFFER YOU A FREE BOOK?
Bill Thompson's award-winning first novel,
***The Bethlehem Scroll*, can be yours free.**
Just go to
billthompsonbooks.com
and click "Subscribe."

Once you're on the list, you'll receive advance notice of future book releases and our newsletter.

Made in the USA
Las Vegas, NV
31 December 2022

64542342R00148